Bought at Provident [illegible] Pa.
on Jan. 24, 2001

Twins

Twins

by

CAROL DUERKSEN & MAYNARD KNEPP

Twins
Book 1 — Skye Series

First Printing, 1997

Printed in the United States of America

Cover illustration by Susan Bartel

Page design & layout by Good Shepherd Publications, Hillsboro, Kansas

Library of Congress Catalog Number 97-61694
ISBN 0-9648525-6-X

Acknowledgements

The following friends, family members, and manuscript readers were invaluable in the birth of *TWINS*. They supported, encouraged, critiqued, and told us what worked and what didn't. Thank you so much to:

Charity Bucher
Mike and Nancy Adams
Brian Bigler
Brenda Cash
Gary Duerksen
Marlo Duerksen
Milton and Alice Duerksen
Mary Lou Farmer
Leanne Githens
Eddy Hall
Cindy Hastings
Myra Jacobs
Steven James
Susan Krehbiel
Laurie Oswald
Jake Schmidt
Chris Scott

And to Julia Brandstatter, our German exchange student who patiently put up with a host mom who lived at her computer—*Julia, please come visit sometime! I'll make you a meal! (Okay, I'll go get pizza.)*

PROLOGUE

JONAS

SOMETIMES—no, many times—I wonder why it happened to me. To me and my family, that is. And if I had been able to see into the future, would I have done anything different? Would I have done more to keep my daughter Becca within our Amish faith? Or was it her destiny to leave and marry Ken? And then the twins … but I'm getting ahead of myself.

I grew up Amish in Wellsford, Kansas. A small, quiet, unassuming farm community. At 16, I ran around with the young folks, like my parents and grandparents before me. I also worked on the dairy farm of a Catholic family and dated their daughter for a while. I learned a lot from them about the world. I learned that there are "English" people who are strong Christians. At the same time, I saw that some Amish people aren't necessarily Christian people. That was a big realization for a teenager who'd grown up believing the way to heaven was through obeying the rules and being a good Amish person.

The thought of leaving the Amish probably crosses every teenager's mind as he or she discovers the fun and conveniences of the world. I was no exception. It was my future wife, Sue Ann, who helped me to see what was right for me. She said, "It's who we are, Jonas. We were born Amish, and that's what we are meant to be. It's all we know."

I guess I believed her with my head at first, although my

heart followed soon after. And if the truth were known, my heart was probably following Sue Ann more than the Amish beliefs at that time, but I was ready to embrace them both. I did, we were married, and I was content.

Becca arrived a year later. What a joy to hold my firstborn in my arms! She had her mother's dark eyes and hair, and I knew I had been blessed by God two-fold.

Three other wonderful children came into our lives, each one of them special in their own way. But there was something about Becca....

Maybe it was the way we could talk together. Maybe it was the fact that she loved the outdoors, and horses, like I do. There was Preacher—the big black horse we raised from a colt. Becca loved him dearly, and I thought she'd never get over it when I finally sold him to be a race horse. I had to, you know. An Amish man can't own a race horse, and Preacher was bred to run. The day after I sold him, I was made minister for life through the lot in our church.

Preacher was no longer on our farm, but Becca had another opportunity to work with horses when she was 16. My brother-in-law Amos in Pennsylvania asked if she'd like to come there to work in his buggy rides business. I could have said no and made her stay home. But I let her go.

Becca did well. Very well. Not only was she good with the horses, but her naturally bright personality made her a big hit with the tourists. It didn't take long for Amos to notice that, and he asked Becca to come back the next summer.

I thought she'd be safe from too many worldly influences in that big Amish community. I thought she might even meet a guy there she'd want to marry.

She did. But he wasn't Amish. Ken Martin was Mennonite. They were friends for a long time, even while Becca dated Amish guys. But for some reason that God only knows, (and I mean that seriously), Becca and Ken realized that they belonged together.

The day Ken asked me for Becca's hand was one of the hardest in my life. Harder even than the day I was made minister. Being hit by the lot, I believe, was God's will for me. But I didn't know God's will for Becca's life. I believed she should stay Amish, but I couldn't force that on her.

I'll never forget the question she asked me one day a few years before she actually left. I'd told her I would feel responsible if she left, and that the only thing I could do was hope and pray that she would find the right way. And then she said, "And Dad, when you pray, will you be telling God what's the right way?"

What could I say?

We were talking in the barn that day, I remember, and I got one of the bridles that was hanging on the wall. I told Becca I believed people need to be wearing God's bridle to give them direction and purpose in life, just like the bridle guides a horse. I told her that for me, wearing God's bridle meant being Amish, and it was most important to me that she wear God's bridle too. I told her I would love her no matter what, even if she wouldn't see things the same way I did.

And that's what happened. She decided to join the Mennonite Church and marry Ken. Even then, it wouldn't have had to be so different. If Becca and Ken would have had children soon after their marriage and she'd given her time and energy to them, I would have been one happy grandfather. But they didn't.

Three years went by. Becca took over the ownership of the buggy ride business. Becca's Buggy Rides, they called it. And a thriving business it was. Becca traveled all over the United States, buying and selling horses. Ken stayed in Blue Valley, Pennsylvania, where he managed the local grocery store. I admit, I wasn't too thrilled with their independent lifestyle, but I know that's how young people are these days.

The weekend of my 45th birthday—I remember it well even though it was more than 30 years ago—Becca and Ken surprised us. They'd been in Indiana buying a horse, and then drove on down to Kansas for my birthday. We had a great time together that weekend—Ken and Becca, our other children Lydianne, E.J. and Emma, Sue Ann and me.

But looking back, the thing I remember most was when we talked about Ken and Becca having children. I teased them, telling Ken what Becca used to say as a teenager: "I'm gonna find me a man that does the laundry, and he can have the kids too." I kidded Ken, and said maybe he just hadn't figured out how to do that yet. He winked at me—I can still see it to this day—and said he thought he knew how to do his part, but he didn't know he was supposed to *have* the babies too. We all got a good laugh out of it.

Light conversation at the time, it was. But I remember it now because of what was to follow. I remember it because the years since have been so unforgettable.

Ken

KEN

ONE

KEN MARTIN leaned on the bathroom sink and frowned into the mirror. Sleep-crud bordered his still-tired, medium-blue eyes, and his nondescript hair stood up horrendously. Why? Why did a person have to look and feel so gross in the morning?

He turned on the water and splashed his face. He ran a short-bristled brush through his hair, sloshed some mouthwash around in his mouth, and padded out of the bathroom. The smell of coffee drifted out of the kitchen.

He needed that cup of coffee this morning. He needed to wake up and somehow put the dream out of his mind.

But who was he fooling, he thought on his way to the kitchen. He wouldn't forget the dream. How could he, when it kept coming back again and again?

"Morning, honey," Ken's wife Becca said from her position in front of the microwave. Ken returned the greeting on his way toward the coffee maker, and Becca lifted a plate of pancakes out of the microwave.

"You want a pancake?" she asked.

"No thanks."

Ken stood staring out of the window, his coffee cup in his hand. An early November snow softened the drab grayness of the Pennsylvania winterscape. The red bird feeder hanging from the tree outside the window hosted half a dozen finches, and more waited their turn in the nearby branches. He'd have to remember to fill the feeder again that evening.

"Are you okay?" Becca asked, looking up from her pancakes.

Ken turned and met Becca's dark eyes. If anything could distract him from the dream hangover, she could. What a beautiful woman, he thought. Even in the morning. One of those women who doesn't need make-up to make you want to get lost in her face and her eyes. How could he be so lucky?

"Yeah, I'm okay," he answered her question. He took a sip of coffee and sat down at the table beside her. "I just had one of those dreams that stays with a person for awhile. You know what I mean?"

"Sure. Tell me about it."

"Not now. We don't have time."

"How about tonight then? Let's go out for a quiet dinner and we can talk. I want to hear about this dream of yours, and I need to talk to you about some possible out-of-state trips in the next few months."

"It's a date," Ken brightened up. "Where do you want to go?"

"How about The Barn? Maybe we can get a stall booth, eat some of their great chili and pie, and just talk."

"Sounds good to me," Ken said, standing up and setting his cup on the counter. "I've gotta get dressed and go to work."

Thirty minutes later, Ken wound his way along the Gary County roads toward the small town of Blue Valley. The first curve he came to brought the dream flooding back to his mind, and he couldn't ignore it.

He would be driving his car, and come upon a curve in the road. In every dream, always the same curve. There, at the side of the road, stood a young woman. Hardly more than a girl, he thought, slowing to a stop. A very very pregnant girl. She opened the door, gave him the once-over, and apparently decided he was safe. She settled into the passenger seat with a thud and a sigh. The contrast between her thin face and bloated stomach tore at Ken's heart. He smiled at her. They exchanged names. She said she was heading toward Philadelphia, and just needed a ride farther down the road.

The rumble of his car's tires on wooden planks brought Ken back to the present. He was crossing through a one-lane covered bridge. Twice a day, every day, he crossed this bridge on his way to and from the Blue Valley. And every time he was reminded of what happened there six years ago. He was 19, and home for the summer after his freshman year of college, when a truck hit his father's car head-on in the middle of that bridge. The truck was driven by an Amish kid who'd been drinking. Ken's father died at the hospital a few hours later.

Becca had been visiting Gary County that summer, working for Beiler's Buggy Rides. The Beilers were their next-door neighbors, so the whole family, including Becca, attended Leonard Martin's funeral. It was the first time Becca had been in a church building, and he remembered her telling him later how different the service was from the Amish funerals she'd attended. She'd been amazed with the way Leonard's life was celebrated, with the music, and with the whole approach to life after death. Ironically, in some ways it was the death of Ken's father that started Becca's thoughts about leaving the Amish.

It was also his father's death that had left him in charge of the family store, Blue Valley Grocery. Perhaps he would have inherited the role anyway later on, when his father retired. As it happened, he finished his two-year A.A. college degree and returned to the business.

Ken slowed down as he neared the speed limit sign outside Blue Valley. The town of 4,000 snuggled under the blanket of snow, at peace for the moment. All that would change, come spring. Beginning with Easter and slowly building into the summer, tourists inched their way along the streets of the town, eager to observe the Amish and purchase 'most anything related to them.

The tourists brought blessings and curses. The cash they left behind supported many families, a lot of them Amish entrepreneurs who'd found ways to cater to the trade. The slow-moving small-town traffic jams were enough to make local people mutter under their breath. Anyone in a hurry to get anywhere on a main road during the height of tourist season might as well take a number and wait. It came with the territory.

But there weren't any lines of cars this gray November morning. The town rested. The locals usually did their shopping on Friday or Saturday, and Ken figured it'd be a slow day. He turned his late-model navy blue Ford into the parking lot behind Blue Valley Grocery, and checked his watch. 7:50. Just in time to open up by 8:00.

♫ ♫ ♫

KEN AND BECCA sat across from each other in a stall booth at The Barn that evening. The refurbished barn included the original horse stalls, which now provided cozy, private settings for customers to eat and enjoy the ambiance. Becca liked the place because of the horsey decor, and the food was always good. She'd ordered a large bowl of chili with lots of cheddar cheese sprinkled over the top, while Ken went for his "standing order" of chicken fried steak.

"I'm dying of curiosity," Becca said, crumbling a cracker into her chili. "What was your dream anyway?"

Ken put a piece of gravy-laden meat in his mouth and chewed awhile before answering.

"First of all, I need to tell you that it wasn't just the dream itself. What's bugging me as much as anything is that I've had it over and over. Many times."

"Like how many? For how long?" Becca asked, her dark eyes studying his face.

"I don't remember exactly when it started. But it's been at least two years already."

"Two years? The same dream?"

"Yes."

"Oh, my goodness! What is it?"

"Okay. I'm driving my car, and I come to a curve in the road. There's a girl—an obviously very pregnant girl—standing along the side of the road, trying to catch a ride. I stop and pick her up," Ken paused and took a drink of tea.

"I ask her where she's going, and she says Philadelphia but she just needs a ride as far as I can take her. For some reason she ends up at our house for the night." Ken looked up from his food and straight into Becca's eyes. "That night she gives birth to twins."

"Twins? In our house?" Becca asked incredulously.

"That's right. Twin girls."

"Man, that is a weird dream."

"There's more," Ken said, getting caught up in the story-telling. "Three days after the twins are born, the girl leaves."

"Leaves? With three-day old babies?"

"No. She doesn't take them."

"She just walks out the door, doesn't say where she's going, and leaves her babies in our house?"

"You got it."

"Unbelievable," Becca said, setting her spoon down and relaxing into the back of the booth. She watched Ken take a bite of coleslaw before asking. "So what happens to them?"

Ken leaned forward, his soft blue eyes inviting Becca to absorb what he was about to relate as he answered, "We keep them."

Becca's face came within inches of Ken's as she reacted. "We keep them? Twins? That just showed up?"

"Told you it was a weird dream," Ken said, almost triumphantly. "Now you know what I mean. And it keeps coming back."

Becca stared at Ken, then slowly dipped the fingers of her right hand in her glass of water. She sprinkled the water on Ken's face and giggled at his reaction, and at her own little joke. "I think you're gonna have to cool it, Ken. These dreams are too much for me to handle. Too much!"

"Well, now you know why I act the way I do the morning after I've had one," Ken said. "I just can't figure out why. Why that dream?"

Becca picked up her spoon again and dipped into her chili. "Do you suppose it has something to do with us deciding not to have children—at least not for awhile?"

"I've thought about that," Ken said. "I think it's possible."

"Do you really want children?"

"Sometimes, yes. But I'm okay with waiting."

"Are you sure?"

"I think so."

"Well, I think your dreams are connected to that. Just so they don't mean that when we do have kids, we're going to have twins. I'm not sure I'm up to it."

"Are there twins in your family?" Ken asked, an ornery smile crossing his face.

"No. Are there in yours?"

"Oh, lots. Lots and lots," he said.

"You *are* kidding," Becca squinted at her husband.

"No twins in my family. Just in my dreams," Ken smiled again, a relaxed, everything's-okay kind of grin. "Nothing you need to worry about."

KEN

TWO

VALLEY VIEW MENNONITE CHURCH hugged a softly sloping hillside on the northern boundary of Gary County. Behind it, the hill rose sharply to a crest, and below, the valley rolled away in waves of fields and forests. In the fall, Valley View's parking lot was a regular stop on Fall Foliage bus tours because the scenic outlook of the valley's multi-colored trees was so awesome.

But it wasn't just in autumn that busloads of tourists stopped at Valley View. The church was one of the oldest in the country, dating back to the early 1700's when the first Mennonites settled in the area. Although most tours focused on the Amish, many guides also gave some background information on the Mennonites in the area as well, and Valley View was a good place to do that. Through the years, the church's pastors and secretaries had come to expect visitors during the week, and graciously hosted them and talked about the history of their congregation.

From the day Valley View was founded, one of the names consistently running through the years of membership lists was Martin. Ken could remember studying the congregation's history when he took catechism class, and being able to follow his family tree to the beginning of the church and back to Switzerland, where his ancestors emigrated from. If the white pillars in front of the red brick church had been inscribed with the names of long-standing families, the Martins would have had their own pillar.

Ken had never known any congregation other than Valley View Mennonite, and for the most part he was content there. Sure, there were squabbles, and some people were easier to like than others. But in times of trouble or sorrow, like when his father had died, Ken knew there was nothing like a church family to wrap its arms around you and carry you through.

Ken was also pleased with the way the congregation had welcomed Becca and made her feel at home, while giving her the space she needed to get used to everything. Growing up Amish, Becca appreciated the sense of community offered by a church, so that part wasn't new to her. The newness came in going to a church building, in the type of worship service, in Sunday School, and in the myriad of church committees and organizations. In the three years that they'd been attending Valley View, Becca had become comfortable with her new family of faith, and Ken was grateful. He wanted Becca to not only feel good about her own church involvement, but to someday share his excitement about bringing up their children in the church.

This Thanksgiving morning, the children of Valley View were bringing smiles of love and pride to parents and grandparents. Ten years ago, the elementary and junior high Sunday School classes had planned and presented a special Thanksgiving service, and a tradition was born. Now it just wasn't Thanksgiving at Valley View without the special Children's Service, and the church was packed. While turkeys cooked in ovens at home, families were led by the children and their teachers in a celebration of giving thanks for God's goodness in their lives.

The service ended around 11:00, hugs and praises were shared all around with the young worship leaders, and then people left for their family celebrations. The Martins would be gathering at the home of their mother, Leanne.

"Mom said Nate made it home, but he slept in this morning," Ken said as he turned into the lane of the family farm.

"I don't blame him," Becca said. "It's a long drive from Kansas. Were there other college kids along with him?"

"Yeah, he had a car full."

"I figured there'd be plenty of kids ready for a break from Menno Simons College. It's just that they spend so much time on the road for the amount of time they're home," Becca commented.

"Don't I know," Ken agreed. "I really liked Menno Simons, but I don't miss the drives back and forth."

Ken and Becca got out of their car and walked toward the white two-story farm home. Behind the house, a large barn and hay shed sat silently, tall tributes to a day gone by. Before his father's death, the farm had been a thriving dairy as well as a bed and breakfast. Leonard and the boys had done the milking, and Leanne ran the bed and breakfast. But when Leonard died and the boys left home for college, they sold the dairy. Leanne kept operating the bed and breakfast, and also went to work as the part-time secretary of Valley View Mennonite Church.

Inside the house, Ken's eyes searched out his brother Nathan. He hadn't seen him since he left for college early in September. When he found Nate sprawled on the living room sofa, Ken let out a loud surprised whistle.

"Oh my goodness!" he exclaimed. "Becca, look what blew in from Kansas!"

Nate sat up and threw a grin at his brother and sister-in-law. He pushed his longer-than-Ken-had-ever-seen-it brown hair behind his ears, revealing a small hoop earring.

"See what I mean?" Leanne said, her voice coming closer as she walked from the kitchen to the living room. "He goes away to college and comes back with an earring. Ken, you've gotta talk some sense into that boy."

Ken's eyes traveled from his brother to his short, plump, conservatively dressed mother and back again. As much as he was surprised at Nate's "new look," he wasn't ready to take sides. No way.

"Hey man, how're you doin'?" he clasped Nate's shoulders in a half-hug.

"I'm great! How 'bout you? And Becca!" Nate grinned

broadly. "It's so good to see you guys!" He stood up and gave Becca a hug.

"What's going on in here?" another male voice called from the kitchen, and a moment later a young man in his early 20's strode into the room.

"Hey Milt!" Nate stepped forward. The brothers quick-hugged, then stepped back and surveyed each other. Milt's hair was as close-cropped as Nate's was long, and while Nate was long and lanky, Milt looked like a defensive end on a football team. In fact, he had been at Blue Valley High four years ago.

"You been lifting or what?" Nate punched Milt's solid shoulders.

"Yeah, I joined the Y. Gotta do something after making chocolate all day."

"So where's my weekly supply?" Becca asked, holding her hand out to Milt. "You promised me when you took that job at More Chocolate that I'd get free samples."

"Sorry! They're really starting to clamp down on employee pilfering," Milt said. "Besides, who needs chocolate when there's turkey on the way?"

"Yes, it's about ready," Leanne said. "If Becca wants to help me get the food on the table, you guys can make sure there are chairs at every place, and decide among yourselves who will say grace."

"No decision there," Nate grinned at Ken. "The oldest one says the grace."

The small family sat down at the oval oak dining room table—Leanne nearest to the kitchen, then Becca on her left, followed by Ken, Milt, and then Nate on his mother's right. "It's good to have everyone here," Leanne smiled wistfully. "But I sure miss Dad," she said, referring to her late husband.

"We all do, Mom, and I'm sure he's with us in spirit," Ken said, then added, "Let's pray."

The family reached out and held hands as Ken prayed. "God, thank you for bringing us together for this Thanksgiving meal. You have blessed us beyond what we could ever deserve, and we ask that you will help us all to find ways to share those blessings with others, whether it be with our time, our abilities, or our finances. We remember the motto that was so important to Dad—We make a living by what we get, but we make a life by what we give. Thank you for enabling us to make a living. Help us to make a life by what we give. Thank you for this food, and be with us in our time together. In Jesus' name, Amen."

Five pairs of eyes looked up, connected with each other briefly, then Ken broke the silence with, "Let's eat!"

The turkey, dressing, mashed potatoes, gravy, green beans, cranberry salad, homemade bread, jam, and mint tea made the rounds. Ken took quick inventory, and said, "Mom, it looks to me like you grew a lot of this meal in your garden, you made the bread, and you got the turkey from the Millers down the road. Am I right?"

"Yes, I suppose you're right," she acknowledged. "It's nice to be able to grow your own food as much as possible."

"That's one thing we haven't taken time to do since we've been married," Becca said. "Summer is the busiest time at the store and the stable, and that's also when a person needs to be gardening. Now, when our work slows down, it isn't very good growing weather," she said, rolling her eyes at the winter scene outdoors.

"Truth is, she's secretly grateful for that," Ken said, looking sideways at his wife. "Becca isn't one of those people who lives to can and freeze produce."

"You're right," Becca admitted. "So, Nate, what's happening in Kansas? Are you enjoying the sunsets and the wide open spaces for me? I really miss them."

"I guess I am." Nate pushed his hair behind his ear again with one hand while stirring his dressing, gravy and turkey all together with the other. "It's a little too wild west for me," he took a bite of his mixture. "No, that's not right. It's a little too west for me, but maybe not wild enough."

"Looks pretty wild to me," Milt reached over and flicked at Nate's hair with his hand. "Long hair and jewelry in the ear. How much wilder do you want to get?"

Nate raised his right arm to fend off Milt's hand, then quickly reached out with his hand and ran it across Milt's close-cropped hair. "I thought about shaving my head, kinda like yours. Would you have liked that better?"

"There's a big difference between Milt's hair and a shaved head," Leanne said in defense of her son. "For pity's sake, don't shave your head."

"What's the difference? About half an inch," Nate laughed. "You all get hung up on such little things."

"You're probably right," Ken said, playing the mediator. He'd grown accustomed to that in his family. He was the oldest, the one running the family store, the married, church-going, doing-everything-that-was-expected-of-him son. Milt was still finding his way, putting in time at More Chocolate and enjoying the single life. Nate was a spirit all his own—incredibly talented in music and art, always pushing the edge with his appearance and clothing, often worrying his mother about what he was getting into while gone at college.

"Oh, before I forget," Nate said, addressing Becca. "A girl at Menno Simons said her dad has a great driving horse he wants to sell, and I promised her I'd tell you. Here's his name and phone number." Nate pulled a folded slip of paper out of his jeans pocket and handed it to Becca. "They live in Indiana—don't you go there a lot to buy horses?"

"I sure do. In fact, I've got a trip scheduled the first week in December. This could be real good timing. Thanks a lot!" Becca said. "Did she tell you how they'd been using the horse?"

"Hey, I don't do horses," Nate said. "I just pass messages on. Sorry."

"You're going to Indiana again?" Leanne asked Becca as she stood up to circle the table with the pitcher of tea.

"Yes, there's a sale that'll have a lot of horses off the track. I've heard it's a good one to go to, and I'm needing to add a couple of horses to the stable."

"Ken, are you going with her?" Leanne asked.

"Not this time. I need to stay at the store."

"So who's going with you?"

"Nobody. I'm doing this trip by myself," Becca said.

"All alone? A 22-year-old woman on the road by herself, pulling a horse trailer?"

Ken had known his mother wouldn't like this idea. He wasn't sure how to reassure her. In fact, as independent as Becca was, (and he liked that about her), this trip concerned him a little bit too. But he'd just have to trust her, and pray that she'd be okay.

"She'll have the cellular phone with her in case she has problems," Ken told his mother. "She'll be checking in with me a couple of times a day."

"I don't like it," Leanne frowned. "I don't like it at all. Can't you find somebody to go with you?"

Ken expected Becca to glance at him at that point, and she did. She loved her mother-in-law dearly, but sometimes Becca's independent spirit chafed against Leanne's ideas of what Becca could or should be doing. Ken smiled slightly at his wife, whose face at that moment was saying, "Come on, Mom, I'll be fine."

"She'll be fine, Mom," Ken said the words out loud, and Becca's eyes silently thanked him. "What about me?" he continued good-naturedly. "I'm the one stuck with a stable full of horses to take care of while she's gone, and I have to have all of that done before I go to work. Is there no pity for Ken the choreman?"

"Oh, poor Kenny," Nate reached across the table and patted his brother on the head. "Shall I stay home and help you shovel horse _____ ?" Nate mouthed the last word of the sentence, but it didn't get past his mother.

"Nate! We don't talk like that, especially not at the table, for goodness sakes!" Leanne reprimanded.

Ken had to hide his smile. He respected his mother too much to laugh at Nate, and what he'd mouthed wasn't appropriate. Nate was a mess, but you couldn't help but like the guy.

"I'll take a rain check on that, Nate, but we'll remember you when we have dirty diapers in the house," Ken said with a laugh.

"Oh! Are you trying to tell us something?" Leanne asked, suddenly hopeful, her eyes flitting expectantly between Ken and Becca.

"No, no, no," Ken quickly countered. "It was just a comment for future reference."

"Oh," Leanne said, and Ken knew exactly what she was thinking. Not only did she want grandchildren, but she figured then Becca would stay home instead of gallivanting all over the country.

Maybe he and Becca should talk about it. At least set some sort of time frame. Yes, he'd mention it sometime soon, when the timing was right.

KEN

THREE

THE FIRST SUNDAY in December, Ken's alarm clock buzzed him awake at 6:00. He groaned as he slapped the annoying noise silent, then sat up in bed. Sunday. Becca was gone. Right. He had to drive to the stable and feed the horses before church. He got up, spent a few minutes in the bathroom, then threw on an old pair of jeans and sweatshirt. When he got to the stable, he'd put coveralls on over everything and he'd be warm—in fact he'd probably be sweating by the time he was done forking hay to the horses. He'd hurry home, shower, eat breakfast and be in church by 9:00.

The horse stable was on the outskirts of Blue Valley—in the opposite direction from their home. Ken drove the familiar road in the dark, meeting no one. The world was still asleep on that starry December morning. Even in Blue Valley, he noticed as he drove through, few houses had lights on.

The time passed quickly as Ken fed the twenty-five horses in the corral outside their barn. He checked the water tank—the electric water heater was working fine and keeping the water from freezing. Becca had commented more than once how nice it was not to have to worry about ice in the water tank in the winter—another of the benefits of electricity she'd come to love since leaving the Amish.

Ken checked his watch as he got back into his car: 7:30. Plenty of time to go home, clean up, eat and get to church. The sun was going to take another few minutes to show up for the day, but it looked like a nice one. Clear, nippy, wind-still.

Driving back through Blue Valley, Ken's mind wandered to Becca. She'd called from Indiana last night and said she bought one horse, and would be visiting relatives today. She'd head back to Pennsylvania tomorrow. He was looking forward to seeing her.

Ken approached the familiar covered bridge that always brought memories of his father. He drove through it, and continued for about a fourth of a mile before he saw her.

Someone was standing on the side of the road ahead of him, just as it curved to the left. The person appeared to be small, yet disproportionately big around the middle.

Ken's heart jumped, raced, and one thought smashed through his mind over and over. It couldn't be! No way! This wasn't happening. Not in real life. Not the dream. No. No!

He felt nauseated, and a chill spread through his body. Without thinking or knowing why, he floored the Ford Escort and flew toward the curve. He concentrated on the road in front of him and on making the turn. Refusing to look to the side as his hands gripped the steering wheel, he took the curve at 60 mph. He didn't know why. He only knew he was terrified, and he had to leave her behind.

The curve behind him, Ken couldn't let up. He had to get out of there, put as much distance between him and the dream as possible. His car raced ahead, toward an approaching buggy—an Amish family on their way to church. To be safe, he should slow down. But he couldn't. He met and passed the buggy in a simultaneous dark-gray blur, and somewhere his logical mind said "They're going to talk about you. They know your car, and they'll talk about how fast you were driving this morning." He wanted it to matter, but it didn't.

The curve, and now the buggy, behind him, Ken was beginning to feel reality returning. Distance and other people now stood between him and the girl at the side of the road. Yes, it'd been a girl. He'd seen enough—he knew. A pregnant girl. But she wasn't his problem. Someone else would stop and help her. He'd go home, take a shower, wash away the cold-chill sweat he could feel sliding down his back. He'd go to church. Someone else would help her.

The Escort sputtered and jerked.

"NO!"

This time Ken's anger echoed loudly through the small car. He frantically pushed the accelerator to the floor. The car had done this several times before—he just hadn't taken it into the shop. He'd always been able to get it going again.

The car coughed again, and Ken's foot pumped desperately. The moments-ago fear returned ten-fold, and a stone thudded into his stomach. No, this really could not be happening to him.

The car gave another cough, one more shuddering jerk, and stopped. Dead.

Ken threw open the door and jumped out onto the roadway. "WHAT!" he screamed. He kicked the tire, then limped to the front of the car. He heard himself curse, and he didn't care. He just wanted out of there.

Panting, he lifted the hood and propped it up. The pounding in his chest seemed audible as he stared at the engine and reached a shaking hand toward the air cleaner.

"Go back."

Ken heard the words even as he felt the touch on his shoulder. He spun around, barely missing the hood with his head.

And that's when he lost it. Tears of anger, frustration, and a beginning resignation coursed down his face. Nobody was there. No human being stood on the road, talking, touching him. Ken leaned forward on the car, his face down, and he began to shake. He trembled and cried because it was the only thing he could do. There was nothing else left inside of him. He didn't know how long it lasted, but finally he stood quiet, spent, empty.

"Go back."

The words, and the touch again. Ken looked up, knowing he wouldn't see the source of the command, or the hand of assurance. He only knew that as surely as he stood beside his car, as surely as the sun was cresting the distant horizon—at that moment God had spoken. And he had no choice but to obey.

Ken fell to his knees on the road, beside the car. He prayed and pleaded, and through it all he said yes. Yes, he'd go back, but oh God, help!

Slowly Ken stood up. The car door still stood open, and he slid into the seat to try the ignition. One turn of the key, and Ken let out a laugh-cry. The engine purred. He wasn't surprised.

Ken turned the Escort around and slowly headed back. A new wave of nervous fright swept through him. He needed Becca right now. He desperately needed to share this with his wife. If the dream was true … if this was the dream coming true, he was driving himself into totally new territory. He was heading down the road to be the father of twins.

No, it didn't have to be that, he told himself. The first part of the dream could be coming true, but that didn't mean the whole thing. It was only a dream, for pity sake. And she was just a pregnant girl needing a ride. He'd pick her up, take her to her destination, and tomorrow he'd be laughing at himself for taking it all so seriously. Yes, that's the way it would be.

Better yet, she's gone, he thought, searching the road ahead of him as he approached the curve. He couldn't see her. Maybe he'd been seeing things all along! Yes! It had all been one very strange figment of his imagination.

Then she stood up. She must have been sitting in the ditch. A young woman, with stringy red hair, wearing a shabby full-length coat that refused to close over her extended belly.

Another wave of emotions struck Ken as he stopped the car. She opened the door, and their eyes met.

"I'm Ken Martin," he said, his voice trembling. "Do you need a ride?"

"Yeah," she said, staring at him, as if detecting the strangeness in his voice. Finally she turned to pick up a small backpack and sleeping bag from in the ditch. She heaved them into the back seat before sliding heavily into the car herself.

The girl—Ken guessed her to be around 18—continued to stare at him with luminous green eyes, then finally she stated matter-of-factly. "My name's Andrea. I slept in somebody's barn last night, and I dreamed someone would pick me up today and help me."

Ken gulped. When he trusted his voice, he asked "Where are you going? What kind of help do you need?"

"I'm going to Florida to have my baby. I have friends there," Andrea answered.

"Where are your parents?"

"In D.C. My dad's a preacher. They had a fit when I got pregnant. I left because I got tired of them ragging on me." She pulled a dirty hair brush out of her coat pocket and ran it through her shoulder-length red hair. "Sorry I look so bad," she apologized. "I need a shower, big time."

Ken's mind was spinning. "How long have you been gone?" he asked.

"Six months."

"Six months! Where've you been staying?"

"Oh, here and there. With friends. Women's shelters. Around."

"When's your baby due?" Ken asked.

"I'm not sure. About a month, I think," Andrea shifted her position. "I'm miserable, that's for sure."

"You're not having twins, are you?" The words were out of Ken's mouth before he knew it.

Andrea looked at him strangely before she replied. "No, I don't think so. Why?"

"Because you're so … big … for being eight months along," Ken said. Okay, it was true, even if that wasn't the real reason for his question. "Have you been to a doctor?"

"In the beginning. When I found out. But not since I've left home." Andrea folded her arms across her chest, and Ken knew his questions were making her feel defensive. But he couldn't stop asking.

"Do your parents know where you are?"

"Not really. I call them about once a month to let them know I'm okay, but that's it."

"Are you going back after you have the baby?"

"I don't know. Depends on how it goes in Florida, I guess."

"Are you keeping the baby?"

"I don't know. I might put it up for adoption. I hear you can get a lot of money for a healthy white baby." Andrea paused, and for the first time, Ken saw emotion in her face. "But I don't know if I can do it," she said quietly.

"It's gotta be a tough decision," Ken said, touching her with his eyes. He wanted to put a hand on her shoulder, but decided not to. He yearned to break through to the soft vulnerable girl underneath, but he couldn't risk it. She had no reason to trust him. Not yet anyway.

"Andrea, if you'd like to take a bath and wash your clothes at our house, you're welcome," Ken said. "My wife Becca is away on a business trip, and I'm planning to go to church this morning. But you could hang out at our house until I get back, and then I could take you to the bus station." Ken was saying the words as fast as they came to his mind. "I'd be glad to buy you a bus ticket to where you need to go in Florida."

"Really?" Andrea's green eyes grew wide, and she smiled for the first time.

"Really," Ken said. "You wanna do that?"

"Yes. Yes I do. Thank you! Thank you very much!"

♫ ♫ ♫

KEN TOOK A QUICK SHOWER and got ready to go to church. He'd thought about staying home, but realized Andrea didn't need him around, and would probably enjoy having the house to herself. He showed her where the breakfast foods were, gave her some of Becca's bubble bath and encouraged her to enjoy a refreshing bath. He rustled up one of Becca's over-sized t-shirts for her to wear after her bath, but had trouble finding anything with a big enough waist for her to wear underneath. Andrea said she'd wash her maternity pants while she was in the bathtub, stick them in the dryer, and she'd have something to wear before Ken came home.

"Until then, I'll wear the long t-shirt," she said, disappearing into the bathroom.

Ken made a quick call to Becca's cellular phone, hoping she'd have it with her. If she was visiting her Amish relatives, the phone would be in the pickup, and she probably wouldn't hear it. Please, Becca, answer the phone, he pleaded. I've got to talk to you. But the phone rang and rang on the other end. He'd have to keep trying.

Ken put on his jacket, picked up his Bible, and walked out the door. He was just getting into his car when he heard Andrea scream. He looked up to see her standing in the doorway of the house.

"Ken!" she cried. "Please! Come here!"

KEN

FOUR

KEN SLAMMED THE CAR DOOR and ran the short distance to the house. Andrea had stepped back inside when she saw he was coming back, and she was waiting for him, sobbing.

"Ken, I'm scared. My water just broke."

"Your water? You mean...." Ken grabbed Andrea by both shoulders and demanded. "How long have you been in labor?"

"This morning," she cried. "Since I woke up. I didn't tell you because I thought it was false labor. Besides, I don't want to go to a hospital. I can't. I don't have any money and I don't want my parents to know. Oh!" she held her stomach and bent over as a contraction hit.

"Well, we've got to get you to a hospital and deal with the rest later," Ken let go of her and hurried toward the phone. His heart was back to thudding and racing again. Just as he picked up the cordless black phone, the doorbell rang. Ken carried the phone with him as he half-ran toward the door and whipped it open.

A woman from their church, Evelyn Shoemaker, stood on the porch. She was holding a foil-covered casserole pan in her hands, which Ken hardly noticed. What did flash through his mind was one word. Midwife. Evelyn was a professional midwife.

"Evelyn! Come in!" Ken said breathlessly, holding open the door for her.

Evelyn stepped inside and started to say "I brought you—" when her eyes grew wide and her voice changed dramatically.

"Ken! Who's this?" Evelyn was looking past him at Andrea, huddled against the wall between the living room and the kitchen.

"Her name's Andrea. She was hitchhiking. I picked her up, and now she's in labor. You've gotta help us, Evelyn!" Ken pleaded, his eyes jumping back and forth between the pregnant girl and his drop-in visitor.

"Well the Lord does work in mysterious ways," Evelyn said, her voice calm again. "Ken, put this casserole in the refrigerator, then go out and get the bag from my back seat. Andrea, you come with me. Ken, is it okay if we use your bedroom?"

Without waiting for an answer, Evelyn took the stunned, whimpering mother-to-be into Ken and Becca's bedroom and closed the door behind them. Then the door opened again and Evelyn called out to Ken, "You can call 911 if you want to, but they won't know any more than I do. I've delivered lots of babies, and we're going to be just fine." The door slammed again.

Yeah. Right. Fine. Just fine. Ken stood, trembling, in the middle of the kitchen, holding the casserole in one hand and the phone in the other. A baby was about to be born in his bedroom. A midwife had just "shown up" in time. Becca was far away. He was afraid again. Afraid of the impending birth itself. And afraid of a birth that could be pregnant with implications for the rest of his life.

He tried to remember the touch and the sound of the words as he stood by his car just a short time ago. God had spoken to him then, he had no doubt. And surely Evelyn's appearance at his door was God's doing too. He wanted to, he had to trust God in this. But oh, he was so scared.

Ken set the casserole in the refrigerator and the phone back on the base. Then he ran out to Evelyn's car to get her midwife bag. He wondered if she had it with her all the time, or if she'd just thrown it in the car that morning.

When he returned to the house, Ken heard a muffled groan-scream come out of the bedroom. He cringed. He'd never heard a woman in pain like that before. The door to his bedroom opened and Evelyn appeared. She took her bag from Ken.

"We're going to need some warm water, a lot of old towels, and a clean towel or blanket for the baby. And, do you have any plastic we can put on the bed, under the sheets?" she asked.

Plastic. Plastic. He couldn't think.

"Like maybe some garbage bags, or a plastic tablecloth?" Evelyn suggested.

Yes, yes, they had a plastic tablecloth. But where did Becca keep it?

"Bring me something," Evelyn ordered, and returned to the bedroom.

Ken began pulling out drawers in the kitchen frantically. No tablecloth. Then he remembered the closet in the bathroom, and ran to look. Yes! There it was. He pulled the red checkered tablecloth down from the shelf, then took an armload of towels out of the closet. He knocked on the bedroom door.

Evelyn took the towels and tablecloth, then instructed, "Bring the warm water and a clean blanket. Andrea says you might as well be in on this, and I could use your help."

Ken returned to the bedroom shortly with the water and blanket. Andrea lay in the bed he was used to sharing with his wife, and it all seemed so unreal. Andrea's red hair and forehead were damp with sweat, and her pale face had turned a shade whiter. Her green eyes reflected fear and ....

Just then, a contraction hit—hard. Andrea cried out, her petite hands pushing down on her extended belly. Her eyes closed, then opened with new terror and pain.

"Andrea, listen to me," Evelyn said, taking one of her hands. "I want you to do three things. First, find something to focus on in this room. Anything at eye level. Focus your eyes and your attention on that. Second, you've got to breathe your way through these contractions. I'll show you how, and Ken will help you. Third, Andrea, listen to me. Massage your tummy in circular motions with your fingertips. It'll help during the contractions. Got that?"

Andrea nodded, and Ken's heart cried for the girl in his bed. No husband with her to coax her through and celebrate the birth of their baby. Only two strangers telling her what to do in the midst of the most pain she would ever know in her life. And he thought *he* was scared.

Together, Ken and Andrea took a crash course in Lamaze breathing from Evelyn. Ken listened to Evelyn and prayed, then breathed with Andrea and prayed. Oh God, help her and the baby get through this okay, he pleaded.

It seemed to take forever. Ken kept a cool wet cloth on Andrea's face, and gave her ice chips to suck on. They puffed and blew together. Finally, after about thirty minutes, Evelyn said she could see the baby's head. The water and blanket were ready, as well as Evelyn's syringe to clear the baby's nose and mouth and the clamp and scissors for the cord.

Andrea had been wanting to push for a while already, but Evelyn hadn't let her. The baby hadn't been far enough in the birth canal. But now Evelyn gave Andrea the go ahead. Crying, panting, sweating, and pushing, Andrea squeezed Ken's hand so hard it hurt. Bad. He was crying, panting, sweating and pushing himself.

"Here it comes!" Evelyn exclaimed, her palm under the slippery little head, then the rest of the baby's body was in her hands. "Andrea! You have a little girl!"

A brand new baby cry answered the hope in the hearts in the room, and then they all cried. Tears coursed down Ken's cheeks as he watched Evelyn clean out the baby's nose and mouth and lay her on Andrea's stomach. He'd heard that watching the birth of his child is the most emotional thing a man can ever do. This wasn't his child, but ....

Suddenly Andrea gripped the sides of the bed and groaned again. Evelyn looked over quickly at Andrea's sweat-drenched face. "Are you having another contraction?" she asked.

"Yes!" Andrea gritted her teeth.

Ken's heart felt like it would simply run away from him. He'd almost forgotten the dream, in all the excitement. And now ...

"Oh my goodness, we've got us another baby coming!" Evelyn exclaimed. "Did you know you were carrying twins?"

Twins. She'd said it. Twins!

Up until now, Ken had somehow still been hoping it was all a strange parallel—the dream and the reality. Even after the words and the touch on his shoulder. Even after he knew God was telling him to go back for the girl. He'd still been holding out that it was just a strange coincidence. And now, twins.

Together, Andrea and Ken repeated the breathing exercises while Evelyn cleaned the newborn and lay her on a bed of towels in a brown cardboard box. Then she returned to the foot of the bed.

"Okay, Andrea, push!" Evelyn said. Moments later, she was holding the baby in her hands.

"Another girl!" she exclaimed.

Without warning, Ken felt weak. Dizzy. Afraid he was about to faint, he sat down on the cedar chest against the wall, and hung his head down low. Too much. The dream. The girl. The vision. The birth. Twin girls. Oh God, too much.

♫ ♫ ♫

KEN WAS DESPERATE to reach Becca. Finally, late that afternoon, she answered her cellular phone.

"Hello!" her bubbly voice answered.

"Becca," Ken said, his voice shaking.

"Ken! What's the matter? What's happened?"

"Becca, I picked up a girl who was hitchhiking. She was pregnant. I brought her for a bath and a good meal. And Becca," Ken swallowed hard, trying to get the words past the growing lump in his throat. "She delivered twin girls in our bed this morning."

Silence. Finally Becca said, "You've got to be kidding."

"Evelyn Shoemaker just happened to show up with a casserole for me, just in time to help," Ken added.

"I don't believe this," Becca said, her voice low and quiet. The bubbly was gone.

"You think *you* don't," Ken replied. And then he told her the story, from the beginning to the end. "We called an ambulance to take the babies to the hospital," he concluded, "but Andrea refused to go. They're small, but the doctor said they're close to full-term and they'll be fine."

"Do they have names? Have you told your mother?"

"Andrea had chosen Skye if it was a girl, so that's what she named the first one. The second one doesn't have a name yet. No, I've been waiting to talk to you before I call Mom. Evelyn promised not to tell anyone until I reached you. How soon can you be home?"

"I'll leave right away. What happens now?"

"I have no idea. I think we should try to get a hold of her parents, but she won't give me any information about them. I suppose we could get the police involved, but that doesn't seem right either."

"Well something has to be done. Who's paying the hospital bill? What happens when they're ready to leave the hospital? How is Andrea going to take care of them?"

"I have no idea," Ken said. And then he realized he'd lied. He did know. As much as a soul can know on the inside, without having any outside proof, he knew.

"Becca, it's the dream. And you know what happens in the dream."

"It can't be. Can it, Ken?" Becca's voice was the one breaking now, and Ken hurt to be so far from his life-partner as the realization hit her. Becca had a long drive ahead of her, alone, to come back to a home and marriage that would never be the same.

"Honey, I love you, and it's going to be all right," Ken whispered. "Just be careful driving back, and we'll get through this together."

"Please pray for me," Becca said, and Ken realized how rarely she spoke those words. Becca's independent spirit didn't ask for help often, and she didn't express her spiritual side freely.

"I will," Ken assured. "And let's both be praying for Andrea, the babies, and whatever God's got in mind for all of us."

"I will. See you soon, honey," Becca said. "I love you."

KEN

FIVE

BECCA ARRIVED early the next morning and for a long time, she and Ken held each other, silently, lost in their shared and solitary thoughts. Then they talked until they finally fell asleep, folded together on the couch in the living room. In a few hours, Becca would meet the girl recovering in their bedroom.

At 8:00, Ken got up and called his mother. She was full of concern and questions about what would happen to the girl and the babies, and Ken could only say he didn't know. His mother didn't know about the dream. No one knew except Becca.

"I'll call my Friendship Circle ladies, and we'll get some clothes and diapers for the babies," Leanne said in her Mennonite, we'll-help-out-all-we-can fashion. "They're going to need some things when they get out of the hospital. And I'll tell Pastor Hurst when he gets into the office this morning. You're going to try to get a hold of the girl's parents, aren't you? Even if she doesn't cooperate?" Leanne's voice was concerned, but the tone was also that of a parent who felt "certain measures may need to be taken whether you like it or not, young lady."

Ken thanked his mother for her assistance, and said they'd be going in to talk to Andrea very soon. He hung up the phone and looked at Becca, who'd come to the kitchen during the phone call. She was leaning against the kitchen counter, drinking a glass of orange juice. She looked like she'd traveled for twelve hours, stayed up most of the night, and slept on a couch.

"Honey, what's happening to us?" she asked, her voice laced with emotional and physical fatigue. "It's like a bad dream."

"I know, sweetheart, I know." Ken put his arm around her waist. "And there's not much we can do about it now except trust God." He paused, then continued. "When shall we call your parents?"

Becca sighed. "I don't know. I think I want to wait until … until we know more about what's going to happen. Maybe this evening. Or tomorrow. I don't even know how to explain it to them."

"Okay, we can wait," Ken agreed. "Let's go see Andrea."

Ken knocked on the bedroom door, and a faint voice said "Come in." Ken and Becca entered their room almost as if they didn't know it. How could 24 hours change everything so completely?

"Andrea, this is my wife Becca," Ken said, walking to the bed. "Becca, you're looking at the mother of two beautiful twin girls."

Andrea smiled and reached out a pale hand to shake Becca's. "Nice to meet you," she said. "I'm sorry to invade your house like this. I didn't plan it this way, believe me."

"It's okay, Andrea, I'm glad we could help," Becca said. Ken saw her eyes scan the room, as if to confirm the unusual events of the day before. Without the babies, without Evelyn, without the tension of the birth in the air, it didn't feel like all of that could have transpired in this room the day before. It felt like yesterday was all just a dream. Ken shivered involuntarily. Yes, it was just a dream all right.

"Andrea, we need to tell your parents where you are and that you're okay," Ken said, standing beside the bed and searching her green eyes. "Don't you think you owe them that?"

A small fire kindled in her tired eyes, and then Andrea turned her head away from Ken.

"I will tell them, in my own good time," she said, her voice rising with defiance. "They want to help me on their terms, so I'll call them on my terms."

Ken and Becca exchanged glances. Andrea wasn't going to budge.

"Do you want to go along with us to the hospital to see your girls?" Ken asked, deciding to change the subject.

Andrea didn't answer, and her face was still turned away, staring out the window. When she did respond, very softly, tears were slipping out of her eyes and wetting her cheeks.

"No, I don't feel up to it," she said. "You go and come tell me about them."

"You still need to name the second one," Ken reminded her.

"I'm open to suggestions," Andrea said listlessly.

♫ ♫ ♫

KEN HAD NEVER before experienced the mix of emotions that swept his soul as he and Becca stood close together, gazing at the tiny twin girls through the nursery window. Soft pink stocking caps covered their little heads, and their finely featured faces twitched with infant dreams. Ken had done this before—gone to the hospital to admire the newborn of a friend or relative. But this was different. Looking at the tiny bundles, his heart hung somewhere between the excitement of a friend and the ecstasy of a new father. They were so perfect, so helpless, so full of promise, so much a miracle, so needy. And most of all, their future seemed so uncertain.

"Ken Martin?" A male voice behind them drew Ken and Becca's attention away from the babies.

"Yes?" Ken turned to see a man in nurse attire, holding a clipboard.

"My name's Dave Wiseman, and I just need to verify some information," he said. "When you brought the babies in yesterday, you said you weren't sure who the responsible party would be for billing purposes. Do you have some information today? An insurance card?"

"No, I don't know much more. The mother hasn't been very helpful, and we haven't been able to contact her parents."

"We really do need to get this paperwork filled out," Dave

said. "I understand the unusual circumstances and all, but, well, I'm sure you can understand our position too."

Ken reached for Becca's hand and squeezed it. He turned his gaze back to the window and the babies, then looked at Dave again.

"We're going to have to assume the babies aren't under anyone's insurance policy," Ken said. "I guess you'll need to bill us directly. At least until we find something else out. Put us down as the responsible party."

"Okay, we can do that for now. Let me get your address and phone number then."

After Dave left, Ken and Becca talked to the nurse who was taking care of the twins. The girls were doing well and would be able to leave the hospital sometime the next week. They stood awhile longer, just looking, lost in their own thoughts.

"Skye. It's different. But pretty," Becca finally commented. "But what about the other one? She needs a name!"

"Andrea said we were welcome to help her with one," Ken answered.

"Andrea," Becca said thoughtfully. "Andrea … Angela. Angela. It might be a good name. It doesn't rhyme, but it kind of fits with Skye."

Ken rolled the name in his mind. Angela. The clear words "Go back," and the touch on his shoulder. The "coincidental" appearance of Evelyn at the house. Yes. Angela was a good name.

When they got home, they told Andrea her babies were doing well and mentioned the name Angela. Andrea's green eyes brightened and her smile told Ken and Becca that both girls now had names.

♫ ♫ ♫

THAT EVENING Becca phoned her parents' neighbor in Kansas, Cindy Jacobs, and asked her to tell Jonas and Sue Ann to call back as soon as possible. Fifteen minutes later, the phone rang, and Becca answered it.

"We're fine—no Dad, nothing horrible has happened to us,"

Becca said, and Ken could imagine the concern on the other end of the line. "But there is something that you need to know about," Becca said. She paused for a moment, then continued. "I was in Indiana, looking at horses, and Ken was here. He was on his way home from choring on Sunday morning. He picked up a hitchhiker—a girl—and…" Becca stopped. Ken watched as she swallowed several times, and her eyes began to fill with tears. "Dad, I'm going to have Ken tell you what happened," she said, her voice shaking. She handed the phone to Ken.

"Ken! What happened?" Jonas's voice on the other end was full of concern. "Why is Becca crying?"

"It's been a bit stressful for her—for both of us," Ken explained. "Like she said, I picked up a girl who was hitchhiking."

Ken went on to explain the events of the day before, realizing how strange they must sound. He included the part about the words "Go back" and the touch, and about Evelyn's showing up. But he didn't tell Jonas about the dream. That could come later. In a long letter.

"And you can't get in touch with her parents?" Jonas asked at the end of the story.

"So far, we haven't been able to," Ken said.

"It's all very strange," Jonas said. "If you'd ask me if I believe in angels, I would probably say yes. And when I hear a story like what you just told me, and it seems that you've had contact with the power of God like that, it gives me the chills."

And you don't know half the story, Ken thought to himself. He almost said it out loud, in fact, but knew then he'd have to explain everything over the phone. And he didn't want to. He wanted to write it down and let Jonas and Sue Ann mull it over together, in their own time.

"It gives me chills too," Ken agreed with Jonas. "Even now. We'll keep you posted on what happens. Here, I think Becca wants to talk with you now."

Ken handed the phone back to his wife and went into the kitchen to begin making supper. He wondered what Andrea would like. He opened the refrigerator and saw the casserole Evelyn had brought over. It seemed like a long, long time ago.

♫ ♫ ♫

THE NEXT DAY, Tuesday, Ken and Becca went to work. Ken didn't look forward to it at all, because he knew the store would be busy. Busy with people coming and going, and they wouldn't be buying groceries either. They would be there to talk about the girl and the twins. Word spread fast in the community, and anyone who could think of any excuse to get to the store that day to hear it from Ken himself would do just that. People would be dropping in at Becca's Buggy Rides too. The gossip mill craved the news, and people knew where to go to get it first-hand.

Of course second and third and fourth-hand information abounded as well. One of the first people in the store that morning told Ken he'd heard that the girl was someone Ken knew, and that she'd chosen to have her babies there. Ken shook his head at the rumor, wondering what other versions of the story were twisting through the tongues of the community. What would really blow them away, he knew, was the real truth. The dream truth.

Around noon, the phone rang at the store. When Ken answered it, Becca's strained voice said simply, "Ken, I came home for lunch, and she's gone. Andrea's gone."

KEN

SIX

KEN AND BECCA sat side-by-side on the edge of their unkempt bed. Intuitively, Becca felt that it hadn't been long since Andrea had left the bed, left the house, just left. She held the note from Andrea in one hand; with the other hand she reached for a tissue. She blew her nose, then leaned heavily against her husband's shoulder.

"I found this after I called you," she said, handing the note to Ken. "Here."

Ken's eyes devoured the neatly printed words on the white paper.

Dear Ken and Becca,

This is the hardest thing I've ever done in my life, but I have to do it and I have to believe that it's what's best for me and for my baby girls. I can't take care of them by myself, and I can't take them home to my parents. Adoption would mean giving them to someone I don't know, and I can't go through that either. I want you to take them.

You are young, wonderful people who don't have any children yet. Please take my girls. Please give them the love and care that you gave me. You are good Christian people, and I can trust you to raise them to be good girls. Please.

You've probably been wondering who the father is. Thank you for not bugging me about it. I know who it is, but I can't tell. I'm sworn to secrecy. Don't worry—he won't come after the girls. Trust me.

I promise you that I will never come back to try to take the girls away. I hope you believe me. I hope you will take them into your life and treat them as your own.

I am leaving a letter for you to give to the girls when they are 12-13 years old. Please give it to them when you feel they are ready—it will explain some things that they should be able to understand then.

I called a friend of mine yesterday, and he came to get me while you were at work today. Please don't worry about me or try to find me. I'm not hitchhiking, and I'll be okay.

I don't know how much I believe in God, but when I had the dream that someone would stop and help me, and then when it happened like it did—well maybe I believe in God a little bit more now than before. I know you believe in God, and I really like the picture on your wall of Jesus holding the lamb. That picture helped me get through the pain of delivering my babies. I believe that your God will help you take care of my girls.

Thank you for everything. I don't know what else to say.

Love, Andrea

Ken laid the letter on the bed and wrapped his arms around Becca. They held each other for a long time, and then Ken thought he heard a small chuckle growing in Becca's throat. He gently pulled away far enough to look at her face. "Yes?" he said.

"You won't believe what just came to me," Becca answered. Her eyes still glistened with tears, but they were on the verge of smiling. "I remembered what I used to say as a teenager, and what Dad reminded you of when we were there for his birthday. I said I'd find me a man who'd do the laundry and have the children. Isn't it strange," Becca paused and half-smiled. "I think the part we all thought was impossible just happened."

♫ ♫ ♫

Ken stood behind the pulpit of Valley View Mennonite Church the next Sunday morning, gripping the sides with white knuckles. His legs shook, and he didn't trust his voice. His heart seemed to be running the hundred yard dash, and his stomach was threatening to return the toast and orange juice he'd forced down for breakfast. He wished he'd never thought he needed to talk during sharing time, but now here he was. And of course everyone expected him to share. Because everyone knew already, but they wanted to know more. They wanted to hear it from him. They wanted all the details.

"A week ago today, I was driving home after feeding the horses," he began. "Just after the covered bridge, where the road curves, I saw a girl who was hitchhiking. She was obviously pregnant."

Ken had the attention of everyone in the congregation, that was sure. Even the kids who were usually coloring or reading to pass the time were listening to and watching him. They'd heard bits and pieces of this story in their homes. The fact that it involved a pregnant girl and the birth of babies in a house made it even more intriguing for the children.

Ken took a deep breath. He'd thought long and hard about whether to tell the congregation what happened next, and finally decided he had to. Unbelievable as it would sound.

"I drove past her," he paused. "I drove past her because I've had a dream that keeps coming back, and it has to do with me picking up a pregnant hitchhiker. I was scared out of my mind, so I drove past her."

Despite all of the gossip circulating in the community, no one knew this part of the story. The intensity among the listeners increased.

"I drove past the girl, but I didn't get very far, because my car stopped on me," Ken said. "Then I was furious. I got out, screamed some words I shouldn't have, and started fiddling around under the hood. That's when I heard a voice say 'Go back,' and I felt the touch of a hand on my shoulder.

"I turned around, but nobody was there," Ken said. He shivered, remembering, and the amazement on the more than 200 faces staring at him urged him on.

"Nobody was there, but I know it happened as much as I know I'm standing here. And I was as scared then as I am now." The congregation chuckled softly. The humor broke the tension, and Ken continued.

"I cried, I prayed, and the words and touch happened again. I gave in. Because you see, I was beginning to understand that this was all some sort of plan of God's, and there was no point in me fighting it. So I got into my car. It started up right away, of course," Ken smiled, and smiles of wonder returned from the congregation.

"I went back and picked up the girl. She said her name was Andrea, that she'd slept in a barn that night, and that she'd dreamed someone would pick her up and help her."

The faces looking at him spoke silent exclamation marks at the news that Andrea had a dream, too.

"She said she was from Washington, D.C., and she was going to Florida to have her baby because her parents were bugging her. I took her home so she could have a bath and a good meal, and I was hoping to be able to find out about her parents and get in touch with them. I was going to leave her at home and come to church, but just before I left, she yelled at me. She was in labor."

Ken was beginning to feel a little less shaky. He'd made it through the first tough part.

"Before I could call 911, Evelyn Shoemaker rang the doorbell. She was bringing me a casserole for lunch, since Becca was gone on a horse-buying trip. I have no doubt in my mind that God sent Evelyn, a midwife, to our house at that very moment."

Ken found Evelyn in the congregation, and met her eyes.

"Evelyn helped Andrea deliver beautiful twin girls named Skye and Angela," Ken said, thanking Evelyn with his gaze. "We took them to the hospital, but Andrea didn't want to go. The doctor said they were small, as she would expect twins to be, but in good condition.

"Andrea didn't want to see the girls after we took them to the hospital, and Tuesday while Becca and I were at work, Andrea left. She'd called a friend and told him to come pick her up. We have no idea where she is, but she left a note saying she wants us to have the girls."

Ken felt his temporary calmness slipping away. The next part was going to be difficult again.

"All of this sounds strange to you, and I know you're full of questions. It is very weird for us too, but I have to say that we are not totally surprised. Because you see, it is following almost to the detail the dream that I've been having for several years. To say that I have known what's going to happen before it does may be more than any of us can face or believe. But in many ways, it's true. At least until the point where we are now. Andrea is gone, and she has left the twins in our care. That's as far as the dream goes. And now Becca and I are faced with reality."

Ken's hands were folded in front of him on the podium, and he took a deep breath. How he wished he could see past the faces and into the hearts and minds of the people listening to his story. Did they believe the twins were an act of God in his and Becca's lives, or did the people of his church family think he was crazy? Were their hearts embracing him in compassion and concern, or were their minds questioning why he didn't just give the twins up for adoption to a family that wanted children?

"The reality is that, if everything works out with the government social services people and our lawyer, sometime this week we will be bringing twins into our home," Ken continued. "As some of you know, bringing a new baby home when you have been planning for it is a significant event. Bringing twins into a house and family that wasn't expecting anything of the sort is a bit mind-boggling."

For the first time, Ken noticed some of the eyes in the congregation leave him. People were looking at each other, nodding, whispering. "You can say that again," they were telling each other. "You have no idea what you're getting into."

"We have no idea what we're getting into," Ken acknowledged the sentiment. "And we're going to need a lot of help feeding, clothing, and taking care of Skye and Angela. They will be coming home from the hospital some time this week. We don't have beds, bedding, diapers—well, we don't have anything. Hand-me-downs are welcome."

Ken looked at Becca, who was sitting near the front of the church with his mother. She'd been more at peace with the whole idea during the last few days. The initial shock had worn off, and the babies hadn't arrived in their home yet to turn their lives upside down. Becca was okay for now. She was sitting in the eye of the hurricane, and before long she'd be out into the tempest again.

"Most of all, we need your prayers during this time of adjustment," Ken said. "If this is meant to be, God will give us the wisdom and strength to do it. We covet your support. Thank you."

Ken sat back down next to Becca, and she reached for his hand. "You did good, honey," she assured.

The sharing time was near the end of the service. Pastor Hurst included Ken and Becca, Skye and Angela in his prayer. The congregation stood for a hymn, and then the benediction. As soon as the worship was over, a small throng of people gathered around Becca and Ken. Some offered their prayers and support. Others said they had baby items they weren't using anymore. Several volunteered to help care for the babies.

It wasn't until Ken and Becca were driving home, replaying the morning and the response they'd felt from the congregation, that Ken came face to face with a nagging thought he'd tried to push back into his mind. His mother hadn't stayed around after the service as well-wishers came to talk to them. In fact, ever since Ken and Becca had told her they'd probably be keeping the girls, her demeanor wasn't the same. She tried to be nice, but it wasn't her usual warm, reaching-out personality. Something was wrong.

His own mother didn't like the idea of them keeping the twins.

KEN

SEVEN

NOTHING IN HIS LIFE had prepared Ken for what happened during the next few weeks. He'd been through stress and distress before, especially when his father died. But then the church community rallied around him and his family and carried them through the unexpected trauma.

What he and Becca faced now was the invasion of their lives by two demanding, adorable, very special babies. And, unlike the unconditional love and support he'd felt after his father's death, Ken was finding out that not everyone was wrapping arms of care and concern around him and Becca. Not everyone thought the twins were sent by God to their home.

It was the hardest to hear from his own mother. She wouldn't come right out and say what was bothering her about it, but she'd throw comments out like "Have you heard from Andrea?" or "Have you had any luck finding Andrea's parents?" or "Are you sure this isn't going to catch up with you someday down the road, like when their father comes to find them?"

Ken didn't know how to handle his mother's negative reaction. She'd been so positive and helpful in the beginning, offering to get her Friendship Circle from the church involved in finding clothes and diapers for the babies. But that was before Andrea left, and Ken and Becca had decided to keep the girls. Leanne agreed to help with the babies when Ken asked her, but she seemed to be doing it out of obligation and because she couldn't say no. Ken watched, and when she held the babies, it wasn't a grandmother holding them, it was someone who felt sorry for them and thought it was her duty to help out. Ken was thankful for her assistance—he didn't know what they would have done without it—but it hurt. It hurt not to see his mother accepting his girls into her heart.

He wanted to ask why, but he wasn't sure he could handle the answer. The stress of helping Becca in the evenings and during the night with the feedings, the loss of sleep, trying to keep regular hours at the store, and feeling the undercurrent among some people in the community—he didn't know if he could add any more to his already overtaxed brain and body. So he didn't ask and Leanne didn't say.

But he wondered. And as he began to hear what the community people were saying, he wondered which attitude matched his mother's.

Some people just didn't buy it. The dream, the destiny. Maybe he had the dreams, maybe he didn't. Maybe he was saying he had the dreams in order to justify what he and Becca were doing. After all, involving an angel and God was a good way to earn empathy. Why he and Becca wanted to adopt a runaway girl's babies was another question, but they didn't have to pretend it was an act of God.

Ken could understand those misgivings. He'd been there. But faith finally outdistanced doubt, and he believed. He'd had no choice there on the road beside his disabled car.

Some people not only didn't buy Ken's story, they raised questions. Who was the twins' father? Why was that information so secretive? Why didn't Ken and Becca try harder to find the girl's parents? Why didn't they turn the case over to social services? Why didn't Becca seem as enthused about this whole thing as Ken? Wasn't that a bit strange? And why did Becca spend so much time away from home buying horses?

Ken had no patience with those rumors. Of course those people didn't talk to him or Becca directly. But the talk filtered into their ears nevertheless.

Probably most of the people who heard about the twins fell into the "we believe but let's be practical" group. If Ken had a dream, and it came true, so be it. God still acts in the world, without a doubt. But maybe what God had in mind was more of a temporary assistance—a place for Andrea to have her babies safely. But adopt them? For life? With so many unknowns? It just wasn't practical. And after all, didn't Ken and Becca want children of their own flesh and blood? In their own good time, not some unexpected "guess what I found on the doorstep" situation. And what about Becca? Was it fair to her for Ken to have his dream, bring the girl home, help her deliver babies in his marriage bed, and then say it was the will of God that they change their lives forever by adopting twin babies?

Ken admitted up front to Becca that he struggled with those same questions. It didn't seem fair to Becca, and maybe his role was to provide a place for the babies to be born, and nothing more. Maybe those people were right—many of them were church leaders, after all. He guessed his mother was in that camp as well, and he could understand that. She believed in the supernatural powers of God—she probably didn't have any problem with the dream. But she wanted grandchildren of her own, she'd told him that many times, and she was probably afraid of the unknown genetics that came with the twins. Ken surmised that his mother just didn't think it was right for them.

Of course there were supportive people too—people who said, "We're with you, just let us know what we can do." People who didn't wait to be asked, but volunteered to help with the babies and who filled the freezer and refrigerator with food. People who donated "two of everything." People who promised to pray.

Into that milieu, Ken and Becca brought Skye and Angela to church for the first time at the tender age of three weeks. According to their beliefs as Mennonites, there would be no infant baptism—baptism was reserved for those old enough to know its meaning and to acknowledge Jesus as their Lord and Savior. But many Mennonite churches, Valley View included, would consecrate children to God as infants, asking for God's presence in the family and congregation that had been given the privilege of molding the young lives. Ken and Becca had asked Pastor Hurst if it would be okay to dedicate Angela and Skye the first Sunday they brought them to church, and he'd readily agreed.

Ken couldn't have been prouder of the two little girls if he'd fathered them himself, and he couldn't stop smiling as he and Becca each carried a tiny bundle wrapped in soft pink into the sanctuary that Sunday morning. It was the fourth Sunday in Advent, and the church was decorated simply but beautifully for the holiday season. Tiny white lights shone through boughs of greenery, and a large Advent wreath and candles presided over the congregation from the front of the sanctuary. A flash of goose bumps swept through Ken as the impact of it all sank in—Advent, the celebration of the Christ-child, God's gift to the world. And here he stood with Becca, holding tiny babies entrusted to their care through circumstances he'd never understand. The irony—well sometimes it was just too much. Ken brushed his hand across his eyes.

Everyone wanted to see the babies, and everyone oohed and ahhed as Ken and Becca showed them the twins. Finally, they sat down in the back row of the church, hoping the babies wouldn't wake up and start to cry just before the consecration.

When it came time for the consecration service, the girls were awake but quiet. Ken and Becca walked to the front of the church, where Pastor Hurst and two church elders awaited them.

Ken noticed immediately that the elders—Simon Brubacher and Anna Hertzler—were smiling. In fact, they weren't just smiling—they were beaming. He'd never seen anyone that age—both were past 70—look so completely ecstatic. He couldn't believe how thrilled they appeared to be to help dedicate Skye and Angela, and his heart jumped to his throat.

As Ken and Becca held the babies and faced the congregation, Pastor Hurst led the people in a litany of dedication. Then it was the elders' turn.

Simon stepped toward Ken and reached for Angela, while

Anna took Skye from Becca. The tall, white-haired man gazed down at Angela, and then looked at Ken. Finally he spoke.

"I have been an elder in this church for many years, and I have offered many prayers to God for the people of our congregation. I have prayed for spiritual renewal, and I've seen it. I have also seen the worst of our humanness hurt each other and hurt God.

"I did not sleep last night. I know there is controversy surrounding these precious gifts of God, and it should not be so. They deserve nothing less than our total love and acceptance. Every child is a gift of God, and our congregation has been blessed with these two."

Simon paused, and his eyes grew moist, and when he continued, his voice trembled slightly. "There is something very special about these two little girls. I felt it during the night, as I prayed to God about their consecration today. The circumstances that brought them to us are an act of God, and I believe it is just the beginning."

Looking down into Angela's bright eyes, Simon slowly laid a wrinkled white hand over her head.

"Angela Bontrager Martin, I dedicate you today in the presence of your parents and your church family. May you grow to have a loving relationship with our Lord and Savior, Jesus Christ."

Simon handed Angela back to Ken and pulled a handkerchief out of his pocket. It was Anna's turn to speak.

One of the oldest members of the congregation, Anna was among the few women who still wore a white prayer covering on her head. Her gray hair was pulled back under her covering, and she stooped slightly. Her body seemed to be giving ground to her eighty-plus years, but her mind hadn't slowed a bit.

Anna cradled baby Skye in her arms, and then spoke as if only to her.

"My dear little one, we know so little about where you came from, and neither do we know what your life holds for you. But I praise my Lord and maker for bringing you to us and to Ken and Becca. You may not know it yet, but God has given you a very special family and a very special church. That will be important, my little Skye, because God has a purpose for you on this earth of ours."

Anna placed a quivering hand over Skye's small head and said "Skye Bontrager Martin, I dedicate you today in the presence of your parents and your church family. May you grow to have a loving relationship with our Lord and Savior, Jesus Christ."

Anna kissed the tiny forehead before handing Skye back to Becca, and Ken's eyes filled. He could see emotions flooding Becca's face as well. And then he looked at the congregation.

From the front pew to the back, from pockets and purses, white initialed handkerchiefs and dainty white hankies were coming out. And Ken saw, beyond the tissues and tears, the eyes of his church family. Many still questioned, he knew. But many also believed. The words of Simon and Anna permeated the sanctuary with spiritual power and authority. That could not be denied.

Ken and Becca began the walk down the aisle, back to their seats. Ken remembered the momentous times he'd walked that aisle—just three short years ago, joyously, with Becca at their wedding. And a few years before that, following the casket carrying his beloved father. Now he walked it with Becca again, and this time they each carried a new life unexpectedly given to them. My, how things could change, and so fast.

Half way down the aisle, Ken saw his mother stand up in the pew where she'd been sitting, next to the aisle. He hadn't seen her cry since his father's death, but she was crying now. For a split second, Ken's heart sank, and then he knew. These were not the sobs of a soul torn with grief, but the tears of a heart deeply touched. Ken and Becca stopped as Leanne stepped out into the aisle. Her eyes bright, her face glistening, and her mouth trembling, Leanne sandwiched in between her son and daughter-in-law and continued with them to the back of the church. Once there, she led them into the privacy of the nursery.

"I'm sorry, I'm so sorry," she cried, hugging first Ken and Angela, then Becca and Skye. "God, forgive me for being so close-minded and selfish. I know now this is meant to be. They *are* your children and my grandchildren, and I love them so!"

It was one of those times when Ken's face hurt from smiling, and his soul couldn't stop praising God. What a Christmas this was going to be!

Dawdi

DAWDI

ONE

THE HOT KANSAS SUMMER EVENING stuck Jonas Bontrager's worn cotton shirt to his back, and he reached for his glass of garden mint tea on the picnic table. Lightning creased the sky far to the west, and he wondered if they'd get rain that night. The fields and garden could use it.

Much closer, lightning bugs flashed their way through the yard, and these innocent insects were the current interest of his daughter and granddaughters. Jonas's 14-year-old daughter Emma had demonstrated the finer points of capturing a lightning bug and sticking it in a jar—a feat that 7-year-old twins Angela and Skye could hardly wait to repeat. In fact, Angela was at that moment heading his way, proudly carrying her small glass jar with one jailed bug.

"Look, Dawdi, I've got one," she said, placing the jar on the table next to his tea. She spoke English except for the word "Dawdi." His daughter Becca had taught her girls the Pennsylvania Dutch word for grandfather, and he enjoyed hearing them call him that.

"You sure do, Angela," he agreed, studying the flashing bug. "And what will you do with him now?"

"I think I'll let him go," Angela said, taking her jar and skipping away.

Never to be outdone, Skye ran up to her grandfather, a fleck of yellow-green luminescence shining on her forehead. "See what

I did, Dawdi," she stuck her face in front of his. "I pulled my bug apart and put his light on my head!"

Jonas chuckled as he responded, "I see what you did, Skye. You know, that bug gave his life so you could run around with his light on your head."

"Yep, he did," Skye agreed. "And I'm going to get me lots more bugs and put them all over me." With that she was gone.

Amazing, Jonas thought. Identical in appearance—beautiful long blonde hair, green eyes, faces that could belong to angels—the girls' personalities were so different. Angela was going to let her one bug go, but Skye could hardly wait to plaster more all over herself.

He wondered, as he had so many times before, what their biological parents were like. He knew so little—only the brief description Becca and Ken had given of their mother Andrea. They knew nothing about the girls' father. The whole arrival and adoption of the twins had been so strange. At the time, he and his wife Sue Ann hadn't known how to respond to Ken and Becca when they called from Pennsylvania with the news. Of course the poor babies needed a good home, what with their mother just abandoning them. And he had no doubt that Ken and Becca could provide that for them. It was just all so weird, and he couldn't decide if the weirdness was good or bad.

Take that dream story for example. Ken was convinced the dream came to him, and then came true, just like in Bible times. When he and Sue Ann heard that story, Jonas struggled a long time with what he believed about it. A part of him wanted to believe it like Ken and Becca did. But another part of him doubted.

And it wasn't the kind of thing he wanted to talk about with the other Amish ministers, or anyone in their church, for that matter. It didn't affect their church, so the other ministers wouldn't have to discuss it and make a decision. It would become a matter of curiosity, a gossip piece, a news item. So he and Sue Ann had struggled alone. They'd told their other children, Lydianne and E.J., about the twins when they were born, and they'd told Emma when she was old enough to understand. Now, at 14,

Emma didn't really seem to care where the twins came from—she just doted on her nieces and loved their occasional visits from Pennsylvania.

The idea grew on him, Jonas had to admit. From the time he and Sue Ann went to Pennsylvania to see Ken and Becca when the twins were a month old, he'd slowly become accustomed to the idea that they were a gift from God, quite literally dropped into his family. Certainly it was easy to fall in love with the identical little girls, and he and Sue Ann's biggest regret was the distance between them. They missed out on so much, living so far apart. But they'd enjoy every moment they could with them.

Like now. Becca, Ken and the girls had flown out from Pennsylvania. Becca and Ken had stayed for the weekend and flown back that afternoon. Skye and Angela would stay for two weeks and then fly back on their own—an idea that nearly drove Sue Ann crazy with worry. Since flying wasn't permitted in the Amish tradition, neither Jonas nor Sue Ann had ever flown, and the idea of putting their precious granddaughters on the plane alone seemed incomprehensible. But Becca and Ken had assured them that the airlines took very good care of children flying alone, and that kids did it all the time. Skye and Angela didn't seem too worried, at least not yet.

Well, he wasn't going to concern himself with it, Jonas thought. He had two wonderful weeks ahead with his granddaughters before he had to put them on that plane, and he was going to make the most of every minute.

The sound of thunder rumbled in the west, and the lightning had drawn closer. It looked like the twins were in for a good old Kansas thunderstorm on their first night away from home.

♫ ♫ ♫

JONAS FLINCHED INVOLUNTARILY as a bolt of lightning cracked outside the house, and the girls beside him and Sue Ann in bed began to cry. Skye and Angela had refused to go to bed anyplace except in their grandparents' room, and Jonas could understand. Their first night away from their parents, and a storm brewing on top of it all. Sue Ann had fixed a bed for them on the floor with sleeping bags, but even that hadn't been close enough when the storm hit. Now the four huddled together in the bed, the light of a kerosene lamp shining from the dresser. Jonas tried to think of something to distract them from the storm.

"I had a horse once named Lightning," he said. "You know why he had that name?"

"No," Angela whimpered. "Why?"

"Because he had a white blaze on his forehead that looked like a streak of lightning, and because he could run really fast," Jonas said. "I got him when I was 16. And you know what I did with my buggy?"

"I bet you drove it really fast," Skye said, cuddling close to Jonas.

Jonas laughed. "Well, I guess maybe I did. But what I was going to say was that I put reflective tape on the back of it so it almost looked like lightning bolts on the buggy. Nobody else had tape like that on their buggy."

"That's for sure," Sue Ann chimed in. "I always knew which was your grandpa's buggy because of the lightning bolts on the back."

"Do you still have Lightning?" Skye asked.

"No, he died a long time ago," Jonas answered, hoping desperately the girls wouldn't ask how. Now would not be a good time to tell them that the horse had been killed by lightning that traveled down the fence he'd been tied to. No, not good at all.

"I have an idea," Sue said, wrapping her arm around Angela beside her. "Let's sing some songs together. What would you like to sing?" Jonas knew the same thought of Lightning's death had crossed her mind, and he deeply appreciated her quick thinking.

"How about 'Jesus Wants Me for a Sunbeam'? Do you know that one?" Skye asked. "Me and Angela sang it in church."

"No, I don't think we know that one," Sue Ann answered. "But you can sing it for us."

"Okay," Angela said, reaching for Skye's hand. "Let's sing it for them."

Jonas had heard the girls sing before. He knew they had unusually good voices. But he'd forgotten how exceptional they really were. There, in the bedroom with the wind driving sheets of rain against the window, with the lightning daring them to be scared and the thunder adding its own form of terror, he felt himself transported on the light soprano voices of the girls. Clear, perfectly pitched, their voices filled the room with the words and tune, the message and the music of a song he'd never heard before and now loved dearly. He glanced at Sue Ann. Her face looked as mesmerized as he felt.

The singing stopped, but not for long. "We know another one," Angela said. "It's called 'How Great Thou Art.' Do you know that one?"

"I think so, but let us hear you do it first, and then we'll join you," Sue Ann said, and with barely a moment's hesitation, the girls began singing the well-known hymn. Jonas had always loved the hymn, although it wasn't the style or type of music they sang in their church services. A chill spread through his body as the young voices carried the old hymn without a falter. These girls were more than a gift from God—they had been given a truly amazing musical gift. He closed his eyes and let himself float amidst the music.

When Jonas opened his eyes at the end of the song, Emma had joined them at the foot of the bed. He smiled at her and said, "Came for the concert, huh Emma?"

"I can't believe how beautiful you sing," Emma said to Skye and Angela. "Where'd you learn to sing like that?"

"Dad teaches us some songs, and so does our children's choir director," Angela said.

"Do you sing a lot in church?" Sue Ann asked.

"Yeah, a lot," Skye answered. "Shall we sing in your church this Sunday?"

Jonas and Sue Ann exchanged looks above the girls' heads. Amish worship services didn't have "special music" like many churches did, so there really wouldn't be any place in the service for the girls to sing. Besides, the congregation members would probably view it as not being humble, as putting themselves and their granddaughters above others.

"It probably won't work in our church this Sunday," Sue Ann answered. "But maybe we can find another time for you to sing."

"Okay," Angela said, and for the first time she sounded sleepy. The storm outside still rumbled, but with much less intensity.

"Okay," Skye repeated, and curled up on the bed between Jonas and Sue Ann.

"I have an idea," Emma said. "Why don't you two come sleep with me here on the floor, on the sleeping bags? We'll pretend we're camping."

Half-asleep already, the twins slid out of the bed and joined Emma on the floor. She settled them in, and within moments they were gone.

"I don't think I need to stay," Emma whispered to her parents.

"No, I think their tired little bodies finally gave in," Sue Ann whispered back. "They've had a big day."

"And more to come," Jonas added.

"Goodnight," Emma said, tiptoeing toward the door.

"Goodnight, Emma." Sue Ann said, and Jonas echoed the same.

Jonas got up and turned down the wick in the lamp until the light was gone, then slipped back into bed. He reached for his wife and curled himself around her back, then leaned up on his elbow.

"You know something?" he whispered into Sue Ann's neck.

"No, what?"

"I'm glad Angela and Skye aren't Amish."

"You're glad your granddaughters aren't Amish?"

"Because I think they could go places with their voices, and they wouldn't be able to do that if they were Amish."

"True," Sue Ann agreed. "But 'going places' isn't necessarily a good thing."

"You're right. But I have a feeling. . . ." Jonas didn't finish the sentence as he lay back on the bed. He said a short prayer, then gave in to the luxury of sleep.

DAWDI

TWO

JONAS AWOKE the next morning to a world refreshed by the all-night rain. Birds called to each other from their territorial trees, and raindrops glistened on the garden plants. A rain like that always made the world happy, but it also made the creek rise. And when the creek came up in Jonas's pasture, it could mean problems.

So, after the twins' late breakfast—they'd slept in—Jonas asked if they'd like to go for a hike in the pasture. They said yes, of course, and the trio set out. Jonas smiled, thinking how they must look—a bearded Amish man in a straw hat, barn door pants and plain pocketless blue shirt, flanked by carbon-copy green-eyed angels in blonde pigtails and bright play clothes. A camera would be nice at times, he thought.

"Where are we going, Dawdi?" Skye asked, grabbing his left hand.

"We're going to see if the water from the rain last night washed out any of the fence," he answered, stopping at the red solar-powered fencer mounted on a post near the gate. He pushed the button to turn it off. If they had to fix fence, he didn't want to have to come back to turn it off.

"What happens if it did?" Angela asked from his right side.

"If it did, we have to fix it so the cows don't get out."

"Oh," Angela said, and then added. "We don't have any cows at home. Just horses."

"Just lots of horses," Skye contributed. "Mommy uses them to give buggy rides."

"Do you girls like horses?" Jonas asked, skirting a clump of manure in the path they were following.

"They're okay, but I like cats better," Skye said. "Our neighbors have a mama cat with kitties and we're going to get some."

"Is that right? Do your parents know about this?"

Skye's "Yes" and Angela's "No" hit Jonas's ears simultaneously, and he laughed. "We seem to have some disagreement here."

"If we bring them home, Mommy will let us keep them," Skye said.

"That's what she thinks," Angela said knowingly.

"It's worked before," Skye added. "That's how we got Butch."

"Butch? Who's Butch?" Jonas asked.

"Our dog. We went to the animal shelter with Daddy and adopted him from there," Angela explained.

"Daddy said if we took him home Mommy would fall in love with him, and she did," Skye stated. "My shoes are getting muddy."

"Yes, that's part of the deal on this hike," Jonas said. "Would you rather go barefoot?"

"Are there stickers out here?"

"Probably."

"Then I don't want to."

"Did you know we are adopted?" Angela asked, looking up into Jonas's face. Her face betrayed no emotions—it was as if she'd asked him what time it was.

"Yes, I know that," Jonas said.

"Daddy says God gave us to him and Mommy because God knew we needed each other," Angela said.

"And he's absolutely right about that," Jonas agreed, noticing they'd reached their first destination. "Let's stop here. I want you to listen to something."

They paused near a small grove of tall sturdy trees—cottonwood trees. Jonas put an arm around each girl. "Now, listen," he said.

Skye finally broke the silence. "It's just the wind blowing the leaves. Is that what we're supposed to hear?"

"Yes, but it's such a pretty sound. Only cottonwood trees sound like that," Jonas said. "What do you think, Angela?"

"I think it's very pretty, Dawdi," Angela said.

"If you put a tree house in that big tree, that would be fun," Skye said, gazing up the tall trunk. "The Lapps have a tree house. We play in it all the time."

"And who are the Lapps?" Jonas asked, walking away from the grove of trees with the girls beside him.

"Our neighbors where we stay when Mommy and Daddy are at work," Angela said. "They're Amish."

Jonas remembered. Ken and Becca had mentioned this family before. He was glad the girls were being exposed to an Amish family and home—at least they knew something about their mother's heritage, even if she had chosen not to stay Amish.

"When we go home, we'll be there almost every day, for the rest of the summer," Skye said. "I like playing there, but I'm glad we aren't Amish. I like having a TV and a computer."

Jonas chuckled, then asked "And what would be so hard about not having a TV or computer?"

"Star Trek," Skye said without hesitation. "It drives me crazy to be at the Lapps when Star Trek comes on, especially since Mom always forgets to tape it for us."

They'd reached the creek, and Jonas could see immediately that the heavy strand of wire was off the insulated poles and strewn among the debris of a creek gone wild for a few hours. "Looks like we have a mess here," he said, standing a few feet away from the sludge of mud. "I remember cleaning up like this many times with your mother. In fact, I remember the time—we were standing right here, and pulling wire out of the mud, when we talked about your mom's uncle Amos inviting her to Pennsylvania to give buggy rides that summer."

"Really?" Angela said, slipping her shoes off.

"Really," Jonas replied. "That summer she went to Pennsylvania and met your dad."

"Can we wade into the water?" Skye asked, her shoes already off.

"Not in the creek. It's still running too fast," Jonas answered. "But you can walk around in the mud and help me pull this wire out."

By the time the fence was back in place, Jonas was almost afraid to take the twins back to the house. Kids and mud seemed to have a magnetic attraction for each other, no matter how clean the children or their clothes started out. There were few spots on Skye and Angela's bodies not covered with gray-black Kansas mud.

"I don't understand," Jonas said, his hands on his hips, surveying the seven-year-olds as they tried to put their shoes on. "How can you both be so full of mud, when I did most of the work and don't look half as bad as you do?"

He saw Skye's answer approaching him, and he knew he could prevent what was about to happen. But for some reason, he didn't try very hard. And when she lobbed the glob of mud and it splattered against his chest, he didn't turn away very fast or reach out his arm to stop her.

It wasn't long before Jonas knew that showing up in front of Sue Ann with the muddy girls was going to be the least of his concerns. Such silliness was to be expected from seven-year-olds. But from a 52-year-old Amish minister?

This time, he was thankful the Amish weren't allowed to own cameras.

♫ ♫ ♫

A MUCH MORE SERIOUS Jonas Bontrager stood in front of his congregation the next Sunday morning in the home of Al and Ellen Keim. The effects of the warm house and the first two sermons, each lasting about an hour, had taken the usual toll on the listeners. Jonas's blue eyes scanned the people seated on backless benches—men in the rooms to his left, women on the right. Like all Amish homes, this one was built to accommodate church services, with rooms opening up to each other so that a minister could stand in one place and be heard, if not seen, by nearly everyone present. Likewise, the ministers could see almost everyone. And Jonas could see a number of nodding heads.

Although Amish tradition didn't allow a minister to use notes during his sermon because he was to speak "the inspired word of God," Jonas had been thinking about this morning's sermon all week. He'd been studying his German Bible, finding passages to read and quote. He'd memorized some of them.

Jonas found Sue Ann in one of the rows of women. Skye and Angela fidgeted on either side of her. They weren't used to two-going-on-three hour services.

"Sue Ann and I have had some very special guests in our home this week," Jonas said in English, immediately catching the surprised looks of the congregation. Pennsylvania Dutch was their native tongue. Sermons were presented in Pennsylvania Dutch, songs and scripture and prayers in German. Speaking English was unusual.

"Our granddaughters, Angela and Skye, have been with us," he continued. "They can understand Pennsylvania Dutch, but I wanted to make sure they were listening. Not to mention the rest of you."

A little ripple of laughter rolled through the house. Including humor in the sermon was just as unusual as preaching in English.

"Jesus said 'Suffer the little children to come unto me, for of such is the Kingdom of Heaven,'" Jonas said, switching to German for the Bible passage. Then, in Pennsylvania Dutch, he continued, "Children are a precious gift from God to us. They have been entrusted into our caretaking. We Amish have a reputation for having strong families. But I want to warn you this morning," Jonas paused and searched the faces in front of him. Not one head was down, sleeping. "I want to warn you that we cannot take that for granted."

Jonas went on to tell stories from the Bible of children who had followed God because they'd been brought up in God-fearing homes, and children who had strayed from God. From the Old Testament to the New, he talked about David, Samuel,

Timothy, and many others.

"And now I am going to say something that is very personal, and it isn't easy for me to say," Jonas stated. "My daughter Becca did not stay within our Amish faith. You all know that. Having her leave is not what I would have wanted for her. But I want to say today that I believe she and her husband Ken are God-fearing people. I believe that God blessed them with two very special children, and it will now be up to them to raise them in the ways of truth and righteousness. May we all take that responsibility seriously. Amen."

Jonas sat down and bowed his head. That's when the nervousness hit. He'd just done something different. Unusual. Perhaps not very acceptable. Amish ministers didn't share personal stories like that. It just wasn't done. Perhaps he would hear about it now, during the time of response. One of the ministers was standing already, talking.

Agreement on the message. No comment about Becca. Jonas sighed, his head still bowed, and waited for the next response.

Thirty minutes later, three ministers had completed their responses. No one had publicly chastised him. It could still happen in private, but that he could handle.

He finally looked up and found Sue Ann in the sea of white-capped faces. She nodded ever so slightly at him, and her hands reached out to touch Angela and Skye beside her.

DAWDI

THREE

JONAS AND SUE ANN weren't sure if the twins were expecting them to keep their "maybe promise" to find a place for them to sing. Kids that age could be unpredictable—one time forgetting something, the next time counting on it. But the grandparents didn't want to risk letting the girls down, and after all, they loved to hear them sing, too. So they invited a group of friends and relatives over for hamburgers and homemade ice cream that Sunday evening.

Included in the group were Matt and Cindy Jacobs, neighbors and long-time friends of the Bontragers, and Jonas and Sue Ann's two other children. Lydianne was 26, married, and had two little boys. E.J. was 23 and still single. He really liked his twin nieces, and kept threatening to move to Pennsylvania so he could see more of them. "Besides," he'd said more than once, "maybe I need to go there to find me a good wife." But he had a good job in Wellsford with a contract home builder and just never got around to quitting and moving.

"Maybe you shouldn't be eating this ice cream before the big concert," E.J. teased Skye as they stood beside the ice cream freezer, waiting their turn to fill their bowls. "I hear that milk is bad for the throat right before you sing."

Skye pushed her handsome young uncle lightly and replied, "What do you know? I haven't heard you sing!"

E.J., who hadn't joined the church yet and was wearing jeans, cowboy boots, and a short-sleeved western shirt, picked up an imaginary mic, shook his face until his jowls rattled, and then looked down at Skye with his best Elvis Presley imitation. "Hey baby, let me sing ya a song," he drawled. "Have you heard the one about the houn' dog?"

"Hey, let's keep the line moving," Jonas said, stepping up to the freezer. "The Bible says there's a time for everything, and this is the time for ice cream, not singing. Plus," he pretended to glare at E.J., "I'm not sure if there's ever a time for Elvis."

E.J. winked at Skye as he filled her bowl for her. "Guess me and the girls are gonna have to go sit outside at the picnic table and do a little concert by ourselves," he said. "It's okay, Dad, we'll skip Elvis. Maybe some hard rock instead," he grinned, and his boots clicked across the floor and out the door.

It wasn't hard rock, but it was definitely music that drew people outside about thirty minutes later. E.J. had gone to his car and brought a guitar to the picnic table, as well as two small oblong boxes. He'd handed the boxes to Angela and Skye, and asked if they could make music with what was in the boxes.

"What is it?" Angela asked, holding the shiny silver instrument up in her hand.

"Don't tell me accomplished musicians like you two have never seen a harmonica," E.J. joked.

"We're not musicians. We just sing," Angela said.

"Hey, you can do both, you know," E.J. said, taking the harmonica out of her hand. "You just blow in it like this, and the notes come out."

Skye already had her harmonica up to her mouth, and was blowing into it.

"How do you play it so it sounds good?" she asked.

"Like this," E.J. said, and began to play a tune.

"We know that song!" Angela exclaimed. "We sang it in school!"

"Really! Then why don't you sing along while I play?"

And that was the music that drifted into the open windows and across the Bontrager yard, bringing people in to sit around the picnic table, listening to what they would later call "the prettiest voices we've ever heard."

Jonas, Sue Ann, and Emma talked about it that night as they sat out on the porch, watching a huge orange ball moon climb its way up the eastern horizon. Skye and Angela were in bed already, much to their chagrin. But Monday was going to be a big day—Sue Ann and Emma wanted the girls to help do the laundry "Amish style" so they'd have that experience, and then they had corn to pick, shell and freeze. This was a busy time of year, and the twins were expected to help with the farm, garden, and household chores as well as have time to play.

"I wonder if their biological mother or father can sing," Emma said into the darkness.

"I wonder too," Jonas said. "Some people are just naturals at some things. Like Becca with horses. Angela and Skye have a natural feeling for the music and the beat."

"Did you see Skye dancing when E.J. played that one song on the harmonica?" Emma laughed softly.

"Yes, I saw it," Sue Ann said. "That one is going to be a handful yet."

"Ah Mom, she just has a lot of spirit in her," Emma chided.

"I tend to agree with Mom on this one," Jonas said. "They are both such sweet girls, but Skye is definitely the ringleader. She's always pushing the edge just a little bit to see what she can get by with."

"And E.J. just eggs her on," Sue Ann noted.

Jonas chuckled. "True. Maybe it's a good thing they don't see each other more often."

"I wish they lived out here," Sue Ann said wistfully. "For one thing, they're at the babysitters a lot—that Lapp family. If Ken and Becca think they both have to work and can't be at home with the girls, then I wish they could stay with us."

"That would be nice," Jonas agreed. "But I don't think Ken will leave his store, or Becca her buggy rides."

"Maybe they needed to hear your sermon," Sue Ann suggested softly.

Jonas didn't answer. Only the sound of the porch swing and the chorus of cicadas broke the evening quiet.

♫ ♫ ♫

The girls' second week in Kansas flew by in a flurry of work and play. Somewhere, amidst it all, Angela found time to spend with her new harmonica. Unlike Skye, she had the patience to work on learning how to play it, and E.J. came over every evening to help her. By the end of the week, she was playing simple tunes, and could hardly wait to show her parents when she got home.

Jonas watched the dynamics between the twins as Angela learned how to play the harmonica, and Skye didn't. Skye obviously hated it when Angela could do something better than she. And when E.J. tried to tell Skye that she could be just as good with the same amount of practice, she got irritated. "I don't like to practice," she huffed.

She didn't want to practice, but at the same time, Skye was envious of the attention E.J. was giving Angela as he taught her. Jonas shook his head at the obvious signs of her jealousy. She'd do things like asking E.J. a totally unrelated question while he was helping Angela, or make fun of Angela's mistakes. It got to the point where Jonas, Sue Ann, or Emma tried to occupy Skye with something else during that time.

The evening before the girls were going to fly back to Pennsylvania, Lydianne and her family and E.J. joined Jonas's household for supper. Jonas wanted Angela to play her harmonica so everyone could hear what she'd learned in less than a week's time, but he wasn't sure how to give equal affirmation to Skye. The fact was, Angela had earned this extra attention, and that was that.

After supper and the dishes were done, the family gathered outside on the porch where the breeze felt good, and Sue Ann asked the girls if they'd like to sing one more time for everyone. The family joined in on the songs they knew, and Jonas's heart filled with thankfulness for the beauty of the music and joy of being together. His only regret was that Ken and Becca weren't with them.

After a few songs, E.J. casually commented that he and Angela had been working on the harmonica together, and would she like to play a song or two? Angela shrugged her shoulders and smiled. "I'm not very good," she said, her legs swinging from the porch swing she shared with Emma.

"That's true, she's not," Skye said from her lawn chair.

"Well, let's see," Jonas encouraged, deciding to ignore Skye's comment.

E.J. had gone into the house to get Angela's harmonica. He handed it to her and smiled. "Go ahead."

Angela put her mouth to the harmonica and blew into it, moving it slowly back and forth across her lips. The tune she played, "The Wildwood Weed" was nearly flawless. Simple, but flawless.

"That's all I know," she said shyly.

"Let me see that," Skye said, standing up and walking toward Angela.

Angela had no more than handed the harmonica to Skye when Skye jumped off the porch and began to run. "Come and get your precious harmonica," she taunted. Angela left the swing with a lurch and took out after her sister, screaming, "You give that back! That's mine! You give it back! You have your own!"

"Girls! Girls! Girls!" Sue Ann called after them. "Skye! Stop!"

But Skye wasn't listening and she wasn't stopping. After several trips around the house, it was as if a light went on in her head, and she made a beeline for the outhouse. She hit the door at a run, flung it open and just as quickly closed it behind her. Angela arrived at the door breathless and crying. "Skye! Give it to me! Skye!" she cried. "Dawdi! Help me!"

Jonas got up from the porch and walked to the small white building. Although their houses had indoor plumbing, most Amish farms still kept an outhouse for church Sundays and other large gatherings of people. Moments before he reached the sobbing Angela in front of the door, Skye stepped out. Her hands were empty.

"Where's the harmonica?" Jonas demanded.

"In there," Skye replied.

"What do you mean 'in there'?" Jonas's voice had grown another notch graver.

"I mean I threw it away in there," Skye said, her green eyes blazing.

A new round of sobs shook Angela, and she clung to Jonas. "Dawdi! My harmonica!" she cried.

♫ ♫ ♫

Jonas and Sue Ann were uncertain how to discipline Skye. Her blatantly mean action certainly couldn't be ignored. But the girls were leaving the next day, and they didn't want the parting to be on a bad note either. They decided to start out by talking with her.

Skye's mouth was still in a pout when the three sat down together at the kitchen table. Jonas leaned back in his chair and addressed his granddaughter.

"Anybody who throws her sister's harmonica in the outhouse must be very angry inside," he said.

Skye stared at the table.

"Let me guess. You were upset because she could play it and you can't."

Skye's eyes stayed down and her mouth shut.

"You know, you and your sister are very much alike, but you are very different too."

Skye looked up at her grandfather.

"There are things that come easily for both of you, like singing," Jonas said. "And then there are things that you do naturally, almost without thinking, that aren't as easy for Angela. Like talking to people. You're good at that, Skye, and Angela is more shy."

The affirmation brought light into Skye's eyes as she listened to her grandfather.

"Angela happened to take the time to practice the harmonica, and you decided not to. That's why she can play it. If you should decide to practice, you'll be able to play just like Angela."

"I hate to practice."

"That's okay. You don't have to. But then don't expect to be the same as someone who has."

Skye's lower lip began to tremble, and soon tears slipped out and down her soft face. Sue Ann reached her arms out, and Skye left her chair to crumple into Sue Ann's lap. Jonas stood up and put his arms around both of them.

They held each other until the sobs subsided, and Jonas handed Skye his big red bandanna. She blew her nose, and looked up at him with watery eyes. "I'm sorry, Dawdi. I really am."

"I know," Jonas said. "What do you think you should do about Angela not having a harmonica anymore?"

Skye blew her nose again, then answered, "I'll give her mine."

"But then you won't have one."

"I told you, I hate to practice," Skye said, and a smile slid across her face. Jonas chuckled, and Sue Ann smiled and kissed Skye's forehead.

Jonas left the room for a minute, and when he returned, he carried a worn but neatly pressed red bandanna. He pulled a chair close to Skye and Sue Ann.

"I want you to take this with you, Skye," he said, holding up the bandanna. "There will be other times in your life when you'll have to cry, and you'll need this. Just remember that Dawdi and Grandma love you so much, and God loves you even more. Okay?"

Jonas folded the bandanna in a triangle and tied it around Skye's neck. "There now, you need to get to bed. You have a plane to catch tomorrow."

"Thank you, Dawdi. I love you," Skye said, hugging the bearded Amishman. "Night-night."

"Goodnight, sweetheart."

BECCA

BECCA

ONE

SHE HADN'T ASKED FOR THIS.

Becca Bontrager Martin's hands flew through the motions of saddling her tall Palomino gelding, but her mind was someplace else. She could saddle Golden without thinking, but it was the thinking that had brought her to the stable in the first place. She needed to get out, to ride, to run with the wind, to think.

She hadn't asked for this.

Sure, most of the time she enjoyed being the mother of twin daughters. From the moment they'd arrived twelve years ago, she'd believed they were a special gift from God. The circumstances around their birth were too strange —she had to believe a greater power was involved. With that assurance holding her up, she'd been able to live through the double-dose of diapers, bottles, childhood sicknesses and scrapes, and know that she—and they—would come through it all okay.

Of course the girls brought infinitely more pleasure than pain into the lives of her and her husband Ken, Becca thought, lifting herself up into the saddle. They were bright—both in personality and aptitude. Angela was the more studious of the two—the one who always got A's and rarely got into trouble. Skye could make good grades if she wanted to, but it just wasn't a priority for her. She'd rather be challenging the guy down the road to a race on their in-line skates. Both of the girls loved music, and everyone in the community knew it. "The Martin

Twins" had been performing since they could say the words to the songs, and Becca often wondered where their natural music ability would take them in life. But right now, they had a very immediate, yet forever kind of problem to face. Skye had just been diagnosed with diabetes.

Becca nudged Golden with her knees and he responded with a slow easy canter away from the stable and down the county road. Becca hardly noticed the awesome colors of the Pennsylvania autumn around her as she and Golden left the road a few minutes later and followed a lane through an apple orchard. She loved this small piece of serenity, away from the traffic and tourists of Gary County, but today she wasn't thinking about her surroundings. She was thinking she hadn't asked for this. She hadn't asked for the girls to come into her life, although she could honestly say she was glad they did. But now this ....

Her twelve-year-old, active, always-pushing-the-limits daughter had diabetes. She would have to learn how to give herself insulin shots. She'd have to watch her diet. No more M&M's—and Skye loved M&M's! No more pop unless it was diet—and Skye hated diet pop. If it had been Angela, she'd have resigned herself and lived with it. But Skye ... Skye didn't resign herself to much of anything very easily.

And on top of it all, the girls were going through puberty. Their emotions teetered between loving and despising, between exuberance and despair. One day they were having girlfriends over and giggling the night away, and the next day they all hated each other. Becca sighed. Had her mother gone through all of this with her too?

In some ways, yes. On the other hand, she faced some very different circumstances with her girls than her mother had to deal with.

She knew so little about the girls' parents. Nothing about their father, in fact. What kind of people were they? What could she expect from the girls? What traits had they inherited? Did certain diseases run in the family?

That's when it hit her. The letter! The letter the girls' mother

Andrea left for them! Her instructions had been for them to read it when they turned thirteen. They'd be thirteen in less than two months. Surely it would be okay to read it now. Maybe they would find out something more about their parents.

Becca turned Golden around abruptly and urged him with her heels. The tall horse was always ready to run, especially if it meant going home. Both Becca and Golden could hardly wait to get back.

♫ ♫ ♫

"Dad and I want to talk to you girls about something before you do your homework tonight," Becca said that evening, standing up from the supper table and taking her plate to the kitchen counter.

"What about?" Skye asked immediately, glancing at her sister.

"They probably found out about—" Angela didn't have a chance to finish her sentence before Skye was in her face, her hand across Angela's mouth.

"Found out about what?" Ken asked, his plate poised in front of the open dishwasher. "Is there something we should know, Skye?"

"Nope, not at all," Skye glared at her sister.

"Angela?"

Angela shook her head, her eyes laughing even with Skye's hand over her mouth.

"Well then, put your plates in the dishwasher and let's go into the family room," Becca continued.

Moments later, the family members had settled into their favorite spots—Ken in his recliner, Becca in the rocker, Skye slouched against a big pillow on the floor, and Angela on the couch with her favorite cat.

"We've told you girls what little we know about your biological mother," Ken began. "We know it's gotta be hard for you not to know more. It's hard for us too."

"Like now, with Skye's diabetes," Becca added. "It'd be nice to know something about you girls' medical history. And that's why we're going to let you read this now." Becca held up the envelope that had been on her lap.

"What's that?" Skye sat up and leaned forward. On the couch, Angela stopped stroking the cat and stared at her mother.

"It's a letter your mother left for you," Becca said. "If you girls want to read it together before we hear it, that's fine."

The words were no more out of her mouth when Skye stood up and took the envelope from Becca's hand. Skye sat down next to Angela on the couch and tore the envelope open.

Becca and Ken watched silently as the girls read the letter. Becca realized—as she often did—what beautiful young ladies they were. Their blonde hair had never been cut, only trimmed, and their unblemished faces weren't fighting acne, at least not yet. One thing Becca knew they'd inherited from their mother was their green eyes—eyes that now devoured the first communication they'd had with her. Eyes that were slowly spilling over onto their fair cheeks. Angela reached for Skye's hand.

Becca went to the bathroom and returned with a box of tissues. She set it down next to the girls, and when she did, Angela handed the letter to her.

"Read it out loud to Dad," she sniffled.

Becca returned to her rocker and began:

My dear daughters,

Where do I begin? There's so much I want to tell you, but I don't know how. I am so scared and confused right now. I'm 18, alone, and now the mother of twins.

I love you. I want you to know that. You might not believe that because I left you, but it's true. I can't completely explain why I did what I did, but I'll try.

I didn't plan to get pregnant. It just happened. Your father is a really nice guy, but that's all I want to say about him. I never told him I was pregnant. I can't tell you the details, but it's just better this way. Please believe me.

When my parents found out I was pregnant, they were of course very upset. They couldn't believe I'd do this to them.

As if I'd gone out and gotten pregnant just to make them mad. Give me a break!

After they got used to the idea, they started telling me what to do. They got real insistent about me giving my baby to some friends of theirs who wanted a child. I didn't like those people, but Mom and Dad wouldn't listen. So I ran away.

I was on my way to Florida because I have friends there, and I planned to have my baby there and give it up for adoption. At least I hoped there I could be involved in choosing the family.

But things didn't work out that way. The night before you were born, I slept in a barn not far from Ken and Becca's place. I started having some pains, and I got really scared. I fell asleep, and I dreamed that someone would help me have my baby—someone I'd never met before but that I could trust. When I woke up, the dream was so real. I wanted to believe it. But there wasn't anybody around, and I freaked. I started to pray—harder than I've ever prayed before. I walked to the road, and I hadn't been there very long when a car showed up. It was going terrible fast, and it flew around the curve I was standing on. It scared me and made me mad—he was driving so fast and I'd hoped it was someone who would stop and help me. Then I had a contraction, and I screamed "Oh God, help!"

Then the strangest thing happened. A voice inside of me said "Don't worry, he's coming back." Over and over it kept saying that, until I started to believe it. So I just sat down and waited.

The car did come back, and it was Ken. As scared as I was, and as much as my mind told me this whole thing was crazy, my heart said it was right.

Ken took me to his house. He helped me through the labor and delivery. And Evelyn too. She was great. Like an angel, she just showed up and helped me have you girls. I think I would have died without them.

I remember, when the labor was so bad I wanted to

scream, Evelyn told me to focus on something in the room. I saw a picture of Jesus on the wall. He was holding a lamb. I just stared at that picture, and tried to imagine myself being held by Jesus like that lamb.

Anyway, we were all so happy when you were born, Skye. And then, within a few minutes, we were so surprised that I was having another baby! Two wonderful little girls!

I was so happy and sad at the same time. Now I'm just sad, because I know what I'm going to do, and it tears me up inside.

I'm going to leave you with Ken and Becca because I don't know what else to do, and because I believe they will take good care of you. They have been very good to me, and I know they will be wonderful parents for you too.

Becca paused because the lump in her throat had grown to the point where she couldn't get past it any longer. She handed the letter to Ken, who was wiping his eyes too. The girls sat close, holding each other, crying softly. Ken continued where Becca had stopped reading.

I don't know if we will ever see each other. You won't be able to find me, but unless Ken and Becca move, I know where to find you. Maybe I will look you up someday. Maybe I won't let you know I'm around, but I'll be somewhere in the crowd, watching the two beautiful twin girls I gave birth to. I know a day will not go by that I won't think about you, and wonder how you are.

I'm not sure what God thinks about me right now, but I hope he doesn't hold any of this against you two. I guess if Jesus cares about lost lambs, he cares about little girls whose mother left them behind. I believe that between Jesus and Ken and Becca, you're in good hands.

I've gotta quit now. I've bawled my eyes out and I don't know what else to say. I love you!

Your mommy,
Andrea

Ken laid the letter down, and he and Becca moved with one heart toward the couch. Angela readily accepted the hug offered by Becca, but before Ken could reach toward Skye, she'd stood up and began walking away. "So, she'll be *somewhere in the crowd*, will she?" Skye threw the words back at her family on the couch. "That'll be *special*—being loved from somewhere in the crowd!"

BECCA

TWO

BECCA LAY NEXT TO KEN later that evening, trying to sleep. Ken was reading his evening devotional, and Becca couldn't go to sleep with the light on. No, it wasn't that, she admitted. She couldn't go to sleep because of the letter, Skye's attitude, the diabetes, everything. She turned over and looked up at the picture of Jesus holding the lamb. Andrea had been in this bed, almost thirteen years ago, staring at that picture, giving birth to Skye and Angela.

"The letter didn't say much about their family," Becca said, still studying the picture.

Ken didn't respond for a few moments. Then, closing his Bible and setting it on the bedside table, he answered, "I didn't really expect it to."

Becca turned a quizzical look at her husband. "Why not?"

"The letter was full of what was on her mind at the time. She wasn't thinking about things like family history, or any of those other details. That's what could be expected from an 18-year-old whose emotions are running strong."

"Yeah," Becca said.

Ken leaned over toward his wife and put his arm around her. "Honey, I know this has been hard for you many times. I'm sorry."

Becca nuzzled against her husband and let him talk. Sometimes she just needed to hear that he appreciated what she was going through. He'd had the dreams and the touch of the angel. Now they found out Andrea had a supernatural experience too. But Becca? She didn't get any of the mystical stuff—none of the out-of-this-world confirmation that what they were doing was right. No, all she got was the down-to-earth details of mothering. And sometimes it got old.

"You're an amazing woman," Ken was stroking her hair. "You hold this family together. When we all seem to be going in different directions with work and school, you're the one who keeps track of it all. You keep your cool with the girls. You run a successful business, and I'm very proud of you."

He kissed her hair, and Becca soaked it up. His lips moved to her forehead, to her nose, onto her lips. She responded with her own kiss, and wrapped her arms around his neck. He kissed her again, stronger this time.

A soft knock-knock-knock drifted across the room from their bedroom door.

Ken pulled his mouth away from Becca's and sighed. "The joy of having kids," he whispered, then lay back against his pillow.

"Come in," Becca said to the door. It opened, and Angela slid in and made her way toward their bed. Becca patted the bed beside her, and Angela crawled in.

"What's the matter, Angela?" Becca asked.

"I can't sleep because I'm worried about Skye," Angela said, pulling her knees up to her chest and hugging them with her arms.

"Why are you worried about Skye?"

"Her diabetes. The way she got mad tonight. Everything."

"I agree. We're worried too," Becca said.

"I've been thinking. I want to go on the same diet too. It's one way I can help her. I won't eat anything she can't."

"Angela! You don't have to do that," Ken said softly.

"I know I don't have to. But I want to."

"It would be good if you'd eat the same food she does when you two are together—which is most of the time," Becca agreed.

"I think I should do it all of the time—not just when we're together. Otherwise I could sneak away and break it, and that wouldn't be right. You know what I mean?" Angela's eyes sought her parents' faces for understanding.

"You're making quite a commitment if you go ahead with this," Becca put her arms around her daughter, "And you know as well as I do that if you tell Skye you're going to do it, you'd better follow through. If you have any doubts at all, it's better not to mention it. You know what I mean?"

"I know, Mom, I know. I'm going to think about it a little bit more."

"You do that, and you let us know," Ken said. "If it's what you really want to do, it'll be very wonderful of you. If not, that's okay too."

"Dad?"

"Yes?"

"When we read that letter from our other mother, she said she was so happy when Skye was born, and then she said she was so surprised when the second baby was born, but she didn't say my name. Why not?"

Ken paused, wondering what to say. He didn't really know the answer, but he suspected ....

"I'm not sure, Angela, but I think it might have been because she had one name picked out, not knowing she was having twins. She named Skye, and we helped her come up with your name. Maybe when she wrote the letter, she just wasn't used to your name yet."

"How did you choose my name?"

"Two very important things. One, it's like your mother's—Andrea, Angela. And because there were angels around that morning."

"You really believe that, Dad?"

"With my whole heart. It's the only way to explain some of the things that happened."

"Sometimes, when Skye and me fight, she makes fun of my name and says I always think I have to act like an angel. That's not true!"

"You act the way you do because of who you are inside,

Angela," Ken said. "You don't ever have to apologize for who you are, especially if you are treating people right and being a kind person."

"She says I'm too nice. She says I don't have any guts."

"Angela. Think about it. Doesn't it sometimes take a lot of guts to be nice?"

Angela's chin rested on her knees. She looked at her father, then mother.

"I suppose so," she answered.

"I can think of one example," Becca said.

"What?"

"You think about it, honey," Becca said. "Now, it's time for you to go to bed, okay?"

"Okay. Goodnight." With a quick hug and kiss for both parents, Angela slipped back out of the room.

Ken looked at the clock, then at Becca. "Now, where were we?" he smiled.

Becca glanced at the clock too and kissed him lightly on the lips. "I think we were going to sleep," she said.

♫ ♫ ♫

SKYE WANTED A CHOCOLATE TOASTER PASTRY for breakfast the next morning, and she couldn't have it. She'd been pretty good the first week since her diagnosis, but she was getting tired of it, and she was letting her mother know that morning.

"I hate this!" her green eyes flashed as she stood in front of the open cupboard door. "I can't eat anything I like! Anything that's good is illegal! Why do I have to have diabetes? And why just me? Why not Angela too?"

"I don't know, Skye, I don't know," her mother answered. "Look, we'll go shopping tomorrow and get some sweet things that are okay for you to eat. It'll just be a matter of getting used to them. For now, how about some cheese and crackers for breakfast?"

Skye slammed the cupboard shut and sulked into the nearest chair. Then she stood up and left the room, returning moments later with the letter from Andrea. She laid it on the table in front of her and began to read it, oblivious to anyone else in the room. Becca silently sliced longhorn cheddar cheese onto a plate and opened a box of crackers. She put them on the table.

Without looking up from the letter, Skye reached for the plate and took some crackers and cheese. She pressed them together—hard—and stuffed one in her mouth. When she did look up, it was with a glare at her mother. "And what am I allowed to drink?" she spit the words out, dripping with bitterness.

"Milk, or orange juice."

"I want chocolate milk."

"Skye, you know better than that."

Skye's eyes flared, and her next words drove daggers into Becca. "I wish my real mother would have never dumped us. I wish we were living with her. She really loves us!"

Becca stared at Skye, her mind spinning. This was the first time either of the girls had said the words "real mother" that way—the first time Becca had heard herself compared to Andrea, and with her coming out on the negative side of the comparison. It hurt.

But Skye was hurting too. Becca wanted to reach out and hold her, but she was afraid of the anger in her daughter. She didn't know if she could help.

At that moment, Angela came into the kitchen and pulled up a chair next to Skye. Becca watched as Angela's eyes took in the situation—the letter, Skye's angry face. Angela reached for the cheese and crackers and ate silently.

The tension hung heavy in the small kitchen for a few minutes. Then Skye stood up abruptly and stomped out of the room.

♫ ♫ ♫

THE PHONE RANG that afternoon at the stable where Becca was doing some paperwork for the business.

"Becca, this is Diana Smith at the school." The voice of the school counselor caught Becca by surprise, and her heart skipped a beat.

"Yes?"

"It seems that Skye asked to be excused to go to the restroom during last hour, and she didn't return. Have you heard from her?"

"No. No!" Becca exclaimed, fear fringing her voice. "What does Angela say?"

"She said she noticed that Skye took her backpack to school with her this morning, which she thought was strange, but Skye didn't tell her anything. She's pretty upset."

"I'll be right there," Becca said. "Have you called Ken at the store?"

"No, but we can."

"I'll meet him there."

Ken and Angela were in the counselor's office when Becca arrived, along with the Blue Valley sheriff. Angela's eyes were red, and she ran to Becca the moment she walked in the door. "Mom, we've gotta find her!" she cried. "I think she ran away!"

"Did she tell you she might do that?" Becca asked, putting her arms around her daughter.

"Not really. But she was mad this morning, and she took her backpack to school."

"But where would she go?" Becca worried.

Ken stood up and walked toward the door. "I'm gonna go look. Bill," he said to the sheriff, "don't send out a search team until I call you, okay?"

Becca and Angela followed Ken to their car and they left the school on the edge of the small town. Ken took the road out of town that led toward their home.

"Where do you think she went? Where are you going?" Becca asked. "Why didn't you let the sheriff start looking?" She wrung her hands. She knew she should try to stay calm for Angela's sake, but she wasn't doing very well.

Ken was approaching the curve on which, nearly thirteen years earlier, he'd picked up Andrea. He pulled the car to the side of the road, got out, and began walking across the tobacco field next to the road. Becca and Angela were right behind him. The late afternoon sun was sinking fast, and what had been a fairly warm

October day had suddenly taken on a chill. Becca shivered.

"Dad! Are we going to that barn?" Angela panted.

"Yep. Skye's been intrigued with that barn ever since I told her that's probably the one Andrea slept in the night before I picked her up," Ken said. "It's just a hunch, but I wonder if she went there today."

Please, God, let her be there, Becca prayed over and over with each step across the stubble-strewn field. She held Angela's hand as they struggled to keep up with Ken's hurried strides.

The dilapidated barn sat on the edge of the tobacco field on what had been a farmstead years ago. Now all that remained was the barn, pieces of a corn crib, and the foundation where the house used to be. The trio approached the old sliding barn doors and slipped in where the doors no longer met in the middle. It was almost dark in the barn, and it took a few seconds for Becca's eyes to adjust. When they did, she didn't see much, but she could smell the years gone by—dust, mice, old hay and tobacco, long-ago livestock odors.

"Skye?" Ken called out. "Are you in here?"

Becca had been so hopeful that when there was no answer, she almost cried out. If Skye wasn't here, where was she?

"Skye, if you had your shot this morning and you haven't eaten anything, you're going to be in trouble," Angela said into the darkness. Becca cringed. How could she forget about the diabetes? That made everything worse!

A movement and a flash of red outside the doors caught Becca's eye. She turned to see Skye standing there, looking in at them.

"Skye!" Becca cried, and rushed through the opening between the doors.

BECCA

THREE

AN HOUR AFTER FINDING SKYE, the family sat around the kitchen table, eating steaming bowls of chili. Skye still wasn't her usual talkative self, so Becca and Ken were trying to know how much to ask and how much to wait for her timing. What they'd found out so far was that she'd gone to the barn straight from school because she "was mad and needed to think."

Becca wasn't sure what all was in Skye's backpack, but two things were obvious—Skye had her portable CD headphones on when they found her, and she was wearing a red bandanna around her neck—the red bandanna Dawdi had given her more than five years ago.

"I haven't seen that bandanna for a long time," Becca noted, crumbling crackers into her second bowl of chili.

"Yeah," Skye said.

Ken and Becca exchanged glances. Skye hadn't even touched her chili. And it was obvious she didn't want to talk just now. Becca hurt, knowing there must be a lot of pain inside of Skye that she didn't know how to deal with. Becca wished she could just make it disappear for her daughter.

The silence at the table grew more and more uncomfortable until Angela finally announced in a weak voice that the Jesus Jam band was coming to Philadelphia and she was wondering if she and Skye could go. Suddenly, angrily, her eyes flashing, Skye shouted, "Are you kidding? Mom would never let us go. Only our *real* Mom would let us do something like that! I want my real Mom!" Skye pushed herself away from the table and ran to her room. The door banged behind her.

Becca stood up to go after Skye, but Ken gently touched her arm and said, "Wait. Leave her alone for now." His eyes motioned toward Angela, who was sobbing silently in her chair. Becca took Angela in her arms and assured her that everything would be okay, even though it seemed hard at the moment.

Becca was close to tears as she and Ken cleared off the table and washed the dishes. When she couldn't hold back any longer and the sobs spilled out, she fell into Ken's arms and just let herself cry.

"She's going through a bad time," Ken said. "You know she didn't mean that about you. She's just confused and upset after hearing her birth mother's words in the letter, and not understanding why she left them."

Some time later, Becca went to the girls' room and gently knocked on the door. Angela was doing her homework in the living room, so she knew Skye was in the bedroom alone. There was no answer. Opening the door, Becca saw Skye sprawled across the bed, her face down in her arms. She went in and sat down beside her, stroking the long blonde hair.

"I brought you a peanut butter sandwich," she said. "You didn't eat much supper, and I thought you might be hungry."

After what seemed like a long time, Skye turned over and sat up. Her eyes were red, her cheeks tear-streaked. "Why did she leave us?" she hiccuped. "Didn't she love us?"

Becca took Skye in her arms. "Honey, your birth mother was very young when she had you. She didn't know how to be a mother to two tiny little girls. She was so young and all alone. She did what she thought was best. I'm sure it was the hardest thing she will have done in her whole life. She did love you. That's why she thought she needed to leave you with us. I'm sorry I can't explain it any better, but maybe as you grow older, you'll understand more."

"Will you and Daddy ever leave us?" Skye sniffled.

"No, Skye, never. We are your parents forever and we will love you forever. No matter what."

Becca held her daughter until she fell into an exhausted sleep. She laid her down and tucked her in, then kissed her gently on the forehead. She met Angela at the door as she was going out, and put her finger to her lips. Angela nodded and gave Becca a goodnight hug.

♫ ♫ ♫

BECCA AND KEN weren't sure what to expect the next morning, but were relieved when Skye ran into the kitchen with her usual exuberance and asked about the Jesus Jam concert.

"Concert? It sounds more like something you put on toast!" Ken said, grinning at his daughters.

"Oh Dad, get real," Skye rolled her eyes. "You mean you've never heard of them? It's a Christian rock band."

"Let me guess. They dress in purple," Ken said. "You know, grape."

"Very funny, Dad," Skye said. "Anyway, can we go?"

"When is this concert?" Becca asked.

"The first Saturday in December," Skye said.

"It could be for our birthdays," Angela, who had just entered the room, suggested.

"How much are the tickets?" Ken smiled at his daughters.

"I forgot, but I'll find out," Skye said, and Becca thought to herself, "amazing how she can open up when she wants something from us."

"I'm dying to go," Skye continued. "Someday I'm going to sing in a band—but probably not in a Christian group," she glanced at each of her parents. Becca knew she was waiting for a reaction from them.

"I don't doubt that you're going to do incredible things with your musical talent, Skye," Becca said.

♫ ♫ ♫

IT'D BE SOMETHING GOOD to do together as a family,

Ken and Becca decided as they discussed the Jesus Jam concert. Plus, they had some ulterior motives. The concert was six weeks away. Six weeks was a long time for a girl learning a new diet. They would take the girls to the concert as a reward for Skye sticking to the right foods. And before she could say it wasn't fair because Angela didn't have to do it, Skye would probably hear from Angela herself that she'd decided to join her sister on the restricted diet.

And that's just what happened.

Two days later, when Becca had a few extra minutes in the evening, she borrowed a Jesus Jam CD cover from the girls. She taped the cover to a six week calendar/chart with Skye and Angela's names on it and a place to keep track of their food, and circled the concert date at the end of the time period. She attached the whole thing to the refrigerator with magnets, and showed the girls.

They teased her about treating them like little kids, but every evening, before they went to bed, the girls stopped by the refrigerator and crossed off another day. And every day, the "Ate right" column sported a big X next to both Skye and Angela's names. Becca offered a quiet prayer of thanks.

♫ ♫ ♫

SIX WEEKS LATER, the twins' Jesus Jam CD blasted through the family car's speakers the entire two-hour drive to Philadelphia. Becca told Ken she thought she'd have the songs memorized by the time they got to the concert, especially since they all sounded alike to her. He chuckled and said, "If you hadn't been Amish, your parents would have gone through the music thing with you, too." Becca admitted he was probably right.

As they climbed the stairs to their seats in the "nosebleed section," (as Skye loved to call and demonstrate it), Angela spotted some girls she knew.

"Look, Skye!" she pointed excitedly. "It's Brittany and Kate and Jill! Remember? From camp!"

"Hey Britt!" Skye responded immediately, jumping up and

down and waving across the row of chairs. "Jill! Kate!"

Angela and Skye wove their way through the seats until they reached the friends they'd made that summer at a Mennonite camp, leaving Ken and Becca standing in the aisle. Becca checked their tickets and noticed they were just a few rows up and to the right of the twins' friends.

"Angela!" she called toward the cluster of jabbering junior high girls. "Skye!"

Angela looked her way, and Becca yelled back, "We'll be up there!" she said, pointing toward their seats.

"Okay!" Angela said and turned her attention back to the group.

When it was almost time for the concert to start and the twins still hadn't joined them, Becca wondered out loud if she or Ken should go get them. Ken stood up and leaned forward, checking out the situation. "There's not much room for them where they're standing because people are filling in the seats. I think they'll come when it starts," he said. "If not, I'll go get them."

The girls did find their way to their seats beside Ken and Becca—after the lights went out. "Mom!" Skye said excitedly as soon as she sat down. "They're going out to eat after the concert and said we should come along! Can we? Huh?"

"Please, Mom," Angela joined in. "We haven't seen them for forever!"

"We'll see," Becca said. "Right now, we're here for the concert! This is the group you're dying to hear, remember?"

The biggest differences between hearing Jesus Jam in the car and being at the concert were the volume and the stage performance, and Becca wondered if she was getting old or what. The volume—even in the high seats of the Roundhouse, seemed to drown out the words, and she wondered if the girls understood the words any better than she did, or if it mattered. As far as the band itself, they looked like they were cut out of the same mold as most hard rock performers. Becca decided that when she started judging people by their appearance, she was definitely getting old and stodgy. She sighed, put her hands over her ears and smiled at Ken beside her. He leaned over and yelled above the noise, "I think the girls owe us one!" Becca nodded.

During intermission, the girls could hardly wait to join their friends again, and they returned with a note from Kate's father, Stan, inviting the Martins to join them at a nearby restaurant after the concert. They decided to go.

Becca breathed a sigh of relief when the band left the stage after its second encore, and the lights came up. Skye and Angela had obviously loved every minute of it, and that's what mattered, but she was glad it was over.

"We're gonna go over with them," Angela said. "Okay? We'll just meet you there!"

"Okay, if you get there first, save a place for us, and we'll do the same for you," Becca instructed. "See you soon."

Skye and Angela merged into the crowd and Becca watched as they found their three friends and Stan. Then she took Ken's hand and they followed the trail of people down the Roundhouse steps.

Outside, Becca took a deep breath of the crisp December evening air as she and Ken walked through the parking lot to their car. "I'm glad we did that—I think," she said. "Although it probably means we'll be hearing a lot of Jesus Jam around the house for the next week."

Ken chuckled and squeezed her hand. "It was a good thing to do for the girls. I just hope they don't expect something like this every month that they stick to Skye's diet."

"No kidding. Our budget and my ears couldn't handle it."

It seemed like a long time before they got out of the parking lot, but finally they were on the street heading toward the restaurant. Becca wondered out loud if Skye would know what was safe to order if they got there first, and Ken said he figured the group would wait to order until they arrived.

Moments later, they were standing inside the restaurant doors, and spotted the three girls with Kate's father. Becca's heart stopped when she didn't see Angela and Skye, but then she realized they must be in the restroom. She and Ken made their way toward the table.

"Are Skye and Angela in the restroom?" she asked.

The looks on the four faces staring at her said it all.

"We thought they were with you," Kate said weakly.

Becca felt the blood leave her face and panic growing in its place. Ken stepped up to the table and stared at the small group. "They said they were coming here with you."

"They were with us," Stan filled in. "But at some point—I don't exactly know when—we looked around and they weren't with us anymore. We tried to find them but we couldn't, so we figured they'd gone back to you."

Becca gulped and gripped the chair she was standing behind. No! This couldn't happen! There had to be a good explanation. Maybe it was just a joke that Skye put them up to. Becca ran to the bathroom and flung the door open, startling an elderly woman who had just come out of the stall. "Sorry!" Becca managed, and ran back to the group.

"Let's go!" Ken said, striding toward the door. Becca was close behind, and amidst a clutter of chairs hurriedly being pushed back, so were the others.

"I'm sure they're in the Roundhouse waiting for us," Ken assured Becca. "For some reason, they got lost in the crowd. They'll be there waiting, and Skye'll say 'Where have you been?' Can't you just hear her say it?"

Becca wanted to believe him, but she found herself thinking the worst. Kidnappers. Her beautiful twin girls in the hands of some perverted guys. Oh God, no! She shouldn't have ever let them out of her sight. Or maybe this was Skye's plan to run away—to go find her mother. Maybe even now they were in a stranger's car, miles away, hitchhiking their way to Florida. Becca's heart dropped and she felt short of breath.

Ken careened into the Roundhouse parking lot and drove up to one of the doors. He and Becca jumped out of the car and ran in. Stan wasn't far behind.

"You go that way, and I'll go this way," Ken indicated to

Becca. "Girls, you check the bathrooms. Stan, find someone who's in charge here."

The crowds were gone, and the only people in the hall circling the area were the ones cleaning up from the concert. Breathless, Becca met Ken on the other side of the arena. No twins.

Together they ran through the short hallway into the arena itself. It too was empty except for clean-up crews. Two lost teenagers would have stood out plainly. And they weren't.

Becca felt herself losing control. The girls were gone!

Stan appeared with a woman wearing an official-looking jacket and a large set of keys. "Can I help you?" she asked.

"Our daughters are missing!" Ken exclaimed. "They accidently got left here after the concert, and they're gone!"

"Age? Description?" the woman asked, reaching for her two-way radio.

"Twelve. Identical twins. Long blonde hair." Becca spurted.

The woman spoke into her radio, asking if anyone in the building had seen the girls. Seconds later, a male voice answered.

"Yeah, this is Mike. I was backstage not too long ago, and saw those girls. They were with the band."

"Backstage?" Becca cried, relief sweeping her body. Ken reached for her and gave her a quick hug, and she could hear Stan and the girls reacting with similar exclamations of surprise and relief.

"I'll take you there," the woman said.

When they arrived backstage, Becca saw something she knew she would never forget. The image burned into her heart and mind, frozen for eternity.

Skye and Angela were sitting on the stage floor, singing, surrounded by the band members. Several of the members were playing guitars—the others simply listening and smiling.

Becca caught Angela's eye, and Angela smiled but didn't miss a note. Not until the song was finished did the girls openly acknowledge the small group who had been desperately searching for them.

"Hi, Mom and Dad," Skye said. "You'll never believe what happened."

"No I won't," Becca ran forward, hugging first one daughter, then the other.

♫ ♫ ♫

BECCA DIDN'T KNOW, as the story unfolded from the girls and the Jesus Jam band, whether she should be astounded or just accept it as another one of the unusual circumstances in the twins' lives. They seemed to be taking it all in stride—more than Becca would have expected.

Angela and Skye were following Stan and the other girls as they walked by the stage when Skye noticed that one of the band members had come back onto the stage to get the drumsticks he'd left there. Skye knew his name, and without thinking twice, she called it out, asking for his autograph. He'd walked over to the side of the stage and bent down to sign his name when he noticed they were twins.

"He just looked at us and grinned real big," Angela recalled. "He said something about what beautiful girls we were. That's when Skye popped up and said 'If you think we're pretty, you oughta hear us sing.'"

Skye giggled and looked at Matt, the band member who'd been on the stage.

"She got me," Matt admitted, and Becca noticed he didn't look quite so wild close-up. "I'm a twin myself, so that intrigued me, but anybody who was brash enough to brag about her singing—well, I figured I should hear them."

"So he invited us backstage," Skye said. "It happened so fast, we kinda forgot about telling somebody."

"We knew you'd come find us," Angela said.

Becca wanted to say "But you can't just leave with guys you don't know." She knew that guys in a Christian band should be okay, but it bothered her that her girls didn't think twice about following Matt and not telling someone. But she'd wait with that speech.

"They sang for us," another band member with long black hair said. "They're incredible!"

The girls giggled.

"I got to play Brian's bass guitar," Skye said. "Now I know what I want for my birthday."

The band laughed while Ken and Becca groaned good-naturedly.

"So which expensive instrument did you learn to love?" Ken asked Angela.

"The sax was neat," Angela said, grinning at the band's saxophone player.

"I'll give you free lessons whenever I'm in town," he smiled back.

"Well, girls, we hate to break up the party, but it's time for us to go. We do want to grab a bite to eat and then we have a two-hour drive ahead of us," Ken said. "Guys, thanks for taking such an interest in Angela and Skye. Believe me, they had us scared to death there for awhile, but it all turned out okay."

"Yeah, it's not good on a mother's heart," Becca agreed.

"We're really sorry about that," Matt said. "I don't blame you for worrying. They're very special girls."

You don't know the half of it, Becca thought to herself.

ANGELA

ANGELA

ONE

"YOU LOOK TERRIBLE," Angela said to her sister, who was sitting with her head in her hands at the kitchen table. The house was quiet except for the sound of a cuckoo clock ticking in the living room. Moments after Angela's pronouncement, the little bird in the clock came out of its door and began counting the hours. Cuckoo. Cuckoo. Cuckoo. Cuckoo.

"I'm going to kill that bird," Skye muttered, sticking her fingers in her ears as the German clock continued through eleven cuckoos.

"It's 11:00, so our folks will be home from church in an hour. You'd better start getting some coffee in you and take a shower," Angela said, walking to the counter and pouring a cup of coffee from the coffeemaker. "Here."

Skye took the cup and swallowed several sips.

"You're lucky Mom and Dad told us yesterday that we could sleep in this morning after prom," Angela continued. "I can't imagine you going to church this morning with a hangover."

"Well I had a heck of a lot more fun at the party than you did," Skye said defensively. "What did you goody-goodies do anyway?"

"Oh, we watched the rest of you make fools of yourselves," Angela chuckled. "It was all the entertainment we needed, really. And then we waited around so we could drive you all home."

"You lead such an exciting life," Skye mocked. "You'll be

happy living here in Gary County for the rest of your life. I can hardly wait to get out of here!" She took another gulp of the strong black liquid in her cup.

"Why don't you come to college with me, at least for a year?" Angela asked. "Kansas is far from home, so you won't have our folks looking over your shoulder. We could have a lot of fun there together—and it's close to Dawdi's. We can see them whenever we want to on weekends."

Skye looked up at Angela, and Angela noticed how bloodshot her sister's eyes were. A dead giveaway, Angela thought. Skye's long blonde hair was a twisted mess, and the aroma of alcohol still hung around her.

"You need a shower before Mom and Dad see you," Angela suggested again.

"I'm going, I'm going," Skye stood up shakily. "And for the record, Kansas is not my idea of a fun place to go to college, and as much as I love Grandpa and Grandma, spending weekends with them down on the farm is not my idea of a rockin' party." She half-grinned—the first one Angela had seen that morning—and left the kitchen. "I'm going to wash away all traces of my good time last night," she called back to her sister. "Mom and Dad will never know."

Yeah, right, Angela thought, pouring herself a glass of orange juice. She took it outside on the deck and watched the birds clustering around the feeder in their backyard. The April morning hinted with the promise of spring, and she smiled as the family cat sidled up to her and bumped against her leg.

Their parents knew that Skye partied occasionally. And they knew that she, Angela, would keep an eye on her sister and keep her out of too much trouble. It was Angela who made sure Skye got an insulin shot if her blood sugar was too high from drinking. It was Angela who took Skye home, got her into bed, and made coffee for her in the morning.

Angela worried about Skye. Especially if they went their separate ways after graduation next month. Who would make sure Skye watched her diet and took her insulin shots? Who would make sure she didn't drive after a party?

She's old enough to take care of herself, Angela told herself. We aren't going to be together the rest of our lives. She's going to have to learn to be responsible.

Angela sat down on one of the deck chairs, and within seconds Spike the cat had jumped into her lap. He pushed his head up against her chin, demanding attention. Angela scratched his head. She'd miss Spike and her parents when she went to Kansas to college. And she'd miss Skye. As much as she worried about Skye needing her, she realized, she needed Skye too. Who was she going to talk to about guys? Who was going to keep her up late at night telling crazy stories? Who was going to make her laugh? Who was going to make her try new things, like styles and colors of clothes she'd never choose herself? Who was she going to talk to about things that only Skye would understand?

Sometimes she didn't know what to do with Skye, but she wouldn't know what to do without her either, Angela concluded.

Angela wasn't sure how long she sat on the deck, thinking, watching the birds and listening to the arrival of spring around her. When Skye came out on the deck, Angela smelled her before she saw her, only this time it was the familiar aroma of Skye's apple-scented shampoo. Skye sat down in the chair next to Angela's and handed her a white piece of notebook paper.

"Thought you might want to read this," she said. Skye still had her coffee cup with her, Angela noticed, before her eyes moved to the sheet of paper.

"You're My Sister," the title at the top read. Angela devoured the typed lines, and the farther she went, the larger the lump grew in her throat. By the time she was through with the verses, tears spilled out of her eyes as she looked at Skye beside her.

"When did you do this?" she said softly.

"It's a music class project," Skye tried to sound nonchalant. "I have to write the tune yet."

"You are amazing," Angela said, her eyes returning to the words. She read them again, slower this time.

VERSE ONE
I look into the mirror and I see you,
sometimes I know how you will feel, even before you do,
we're two of a kind and yet we're different in so many ways,
and I am proud to say, you're my sister.

CHORUS
With God upon our side, we made it, you and I,
and we wouldn't change a single thing
for all the stars in the sky;
and if tomorrow comes too fast,
make each moment last today
and the good Lord will remain to lead the way.

VERSE TWO
We'll beat the odds again, I am sure
I hope this world gives you everything you want and more
We're separate lives here on earth
but two hearts joined together at birth
and you can have my shoulder when you hurt.

Angela handed the sheet back to Skye. "I can hardly wait to hear the music," she said quietly.

"You won't have to wait very long," Skye half-laughed. "It's due tomorrow."

Angela just shook her head. Leave it to Skye to leave it to the last minute. And she'd pull it off too. The teacher would rant and rave about how creative her song was, and Skye would just shrug it off. "It's no big deal," she'd say.

But Angela knew better. Angela knew that Skye was dying to be a singer/songwriter/performer, and she was packing every bit of affirmation and encouragement into her heart to take out into the world with her after graduation. It was one of those things sis-

---

"You're My Sister," © 1997 Jake Schmidt/Matthew Jordan. For information on ordering a tape of the song, see page 186.

ters knew about each other without ever saying the words.

The sliding patio doors behind them opened, and the girls' parents stepped out onto the deck. Angela looked around, smiled at them, and asked, "So how was church? Did we miss anything?"

"You missed seeing all of the other youth who made it to church the morning after prom," Ken said, walking up behind Skye and rubbing her shoulders.

"You're kidding," Skye said. "Who was there?"

"Paul. Paul was there," Becca answered, standing beside Angela's chair.

"And he was 'all of the other youth', huh dad?" Skye said, turning around to face her father.

"I sure thought I saw a whole bunch of kids," Ken feigned innocence.

"He's giving you a bad time, girls," Becca admitted. "Paul was the only one there—I guess everybody else was sleeping in like you two."

"So how *was* prom?" Ken wanted to know.

"Okay," Skye said noncommitally.

Ken looked at this wife. "It's another one of those long descriptive answers."

"Did you have a live band or a DJ for the dance?" Becca asked.

"It was a band, if you could call it that," Skye answered.

"And how about the party afterwards?"

"The usual—food, videos, stuff," Skye said, watching her sister closely.

"This was at the city hall?"

"Yeah," Angela said, and her conscience pricked her hard. The party at the city hall had ended at 1:00. After that, a bunch of the kids had gone to one of the the senior's homes, including her and Skye. That's where the alcohol had been.

"Well, we got an exciting phone call last night," Becca changed the subject. "How would you like to have Dawdis here for your graduation?"

"Really?" Angela exclaimed. "Are they coming?"

"It seems there's a van coming this way about that time and they can catch a ride. They said they couldn't miss the chance to come see us."

"It seems like a long time since we've seen Grandpa and Grandma," Angela mused. "But I guess it was just last summer. It'll be neat to have them here!"

Angela loved her Amish grandparents dearly, and the two weeks she and Skye spent with them every summer in Kansas was always a highlight. But they didn't come to Pennsylvania very often, and it would be a treat to have them around for a while. She could hardly wait.

"That's only a month away," Becca said. "We have some major housecleaning to do before then."

The girls both groaned, and Ken chuckled. "Remember, your mother grew up cleaning the house from top to bottom for church," he said. "Now that she doesn't have to do it for church, she needs another excuse."

"I don't need an excuse—the house needs a thorough cleaning!" Becca defended herself. "It just doesn't happen unless we're getting company like my parents. I'm sure Mom will notice everything."

"She won't care," Angela said.

"Oh yes she will. She'll think she failed in teaching me how to keep house."

"Honey, you're forty years old—you don't need to worry about what your mother thinks about your housekeeping," Ken touched Becca lightly on the arm. "But we'll help you tidy it up a bit, won't we girls?"

The girls groaned, and Skye said, "I'm starved. What's for lunch?"

♫ ♫ ♫

THAT AFTERNOON, Skye retreated to the room she and Angela shared, and got her guitar out. Angela was writing a research paper on the computer.

"Is it going to bother you if I pick around on the guitar and try to write this song?" Skye wondered.

"I don't think so," Angela said. "I'll let you know if it does."

"I don't want to work on this in the family room," Skye said. "Mom and Dad are always so curious when I write a song. I need some space—you know?"

"I know," Angela agreed, turning in her chair to face her sister. "It's the same when you and I are practicing for a program someplace. They want to be *so helpful* when there's really not much they can do."

"We know a lot more about music than they do," Skye said. "Do you think our biological mother was musical?"

"I've thought about that so much, and I wish I knew," Angela said. "I wish she'd written more in that letter she left us."

"I wish we could meet her," Skye said wistfully.

"Maybe we will," Angela. "She did say maybe she'd look us up someday."

"Yeah, and she also said maybe she wouldn't even let us know she's around," Skye's voice was bitter now. "What kind of a mother is that?"

Angela didn't know what to say. At times, she felt the same hurt and bitterness. It was one of those mysteries she felt life had given her, and she had to make the best of it. Angela could find peace despite the pain. But not Skye. No, Skye carried it with her. Maybe that's why she was always pushing the edge, partying, looking for happiness outside of herself. When she had a chance, like last night, she tried to smother her anguish with alcohol.

"Not much of one," Angela heard Skye answering her own question. "Well, at least I have you. So, let's write a tune to go with these words."

ANGELA

TWO

ANGELA STOOD IN FRONT OF THE MIRROR in the girls' locker room at Blue Valley High School and adjusted the royal blue cap on her head. She couldn't believe graduation day was here. The weeks since prom had just flown past, and more than once she'd wished time would slow down. Unlike most of her classmates, and certainly her sister, Angela wasn't overly anxious for her high school days to be over. Sure, she was looking forward to the summer break, and then going to Menno Simons College in the fall. But she'd miss her classmates, her parents, and Skye.

Skye. Angela could hear her now, giggling with some of the other girls near their lockers. On a dare, some of the girls had decided to wear shorts and halter tops underneath their robes, and of course Skye was in on it. She'd left home wearing a dress, as had Angela. But when they arrived at the school, Skye's dress got exchanged for what she'd brought in her gym bag. "The robes are long anyway, and it's hot in that gymnasium," Skye had told Angela.

Angela walked toward the group of girls and up to Skye. "Is my cap okay?" she asked, searching her sister's bright green eyes.

"Looks fine to me," Skye answered. "How about mine?" Her eyes were laughing, and Angela knew exactly why. A gummy worm was sticking its head out from underneath Skye's cap, just above her eyebrows. Angela couldn't help but laugh too. "Mom and Dad will kill you," she said.

"Maybe they won't see it," Skye said. "Besides, what're they going to do?"

She had a point. Skye usually knew just how far to push before she'd get in trouble. And when she did, she counted on Angela to bail her out.

But not for much longer, Angela thought. Skye wasn't changing her mind at all about going to college. If anything, she was talking more and more about leaving Gary County and going to New York to try to find work with a band. Angela knew Skye was very talented, but it seemed like a long shot. That reminded her....

"Where's your guitar?" Angela asked Skye.

"Here," Skye motioned. "You taking your violin and putting it on the stage? Will you take my guitar too?"

"Sure," Angela agreed.

"It's time to take the class picture," a male voice yelled into the locker room. "Let's go, girls!"

Angela quickly took the guitar and violin onto the stage before the class assembled for their picture. People were starting to fill the bleachers and chairs set up in the high school gym.

Amidst the expected amount of clowning around, "rabbit ears," and silly faces, the class picture finally got onto film. Angela glanced at Skye beside her and yes, the gummy worm was still there.

The class marched in to the traditional "Processional" song. Angela was ahead of Skye, and she was sure she heard a snicker from the crowd as Skye marched by. She wondered what her Amish grandparents were thinking.

The program that evening would include presenting awards, scholarships, a speaker, and a musical number, in addition to the granting of diplomas. When he'd heard Skye's song, the high school music teacher had decided that "You're My Sister" had to be performed by the twins at their graduation. No one had argued with his decision, including the girls. They were used to being asked to sing in front of groups.

When it came time for the song, Mr. Toews, the music

teacher, strode to the podium, gazed out over the audience, then looked down at Skye and Angela.

"We have a unique set of twins in this graduating class," he began. "Skye and Angela Martin are bright, wonderful young people with a gift for music unlike any I've seen during my twenty years of teaching. Not only do they have outstanding voices, but they can each play several instruments, and they write music as well. The song they are going to share with you this evening was written by Skye for a music class project. It's called 'You're My Sister.'"

Angela and Skye walked up the stairs and onto the stage, picking up their instruments on the way to the microphones. Their eyes met as they stood in front of the mics, and a smile spread across Angela's face. The worm had mysteriously disappeared.

"Like Mr. Toews said, I wrote this song for a class project," Skye said into the microphone. "Just so you know I don't get all sentimental about my sister just for the heck of it—remember—this was an assignment!"

A chuckle swept through the audience, and when it was quiet again, Skye added, "Seriously, I meant every word of this song. Angela is my sister, my best friend, my connection with goodness and life. I admire her and love her very much. Angela, this one's for you." And with those words, Skye began to pick the tune on her guitar and to sing.

I look into the mirror and I see you,
sometimes I know how you feel, even before you do,
we're two of a kind, and yet we're different in so many ways,
and I am proud to say, you're my sister.

Angela joined Skye on the chorus.

With God upon our side, we made it, you and I,
and we wouldn't change a single thing
for all the stars in the sky;

And if tomorrow comes too fast,
make each moment last today
and the good Lord will remain to lead the way.

Angela sang the second verse alone, and after they did the chorus together, the twins spoke through their instruments. The sweet, mellow tune took on a melancholy, almost haunting sound through Angela's violin, and Skye's backup on the guitar was perfect. They repeated the chorus one more time, and then the song was over.

A wave of applause rolled through the audience and over the girls standing on the stage. Angela said "thank you," but she knew it wasn't very audible over the enthusiastic clapping. She looked at Skye, and they grinned at each other. They bowed together as the applause continued, and when it finally ended, they put their instruments away and left the stage.

Seated again, Angela looked at Skye, who was fiddling with her hat. The worm was coming back.

"Why'd you put it away for the song?" Angela whispered.

"It's a serious song," Skye said, and her green eyes smiled. Angela just shook her head. Commencement wasn't serious, but the song was. Coming from Skye, Angela guessed it didn't surprise her much at all.

Neither was it a surprise to anyone when the girls received several prestigious music awards and scholarships. Menno Simons College was giving both of them $5000 music scholarships, but only one of them would be used, Angela knew. It would take a minor miracle for Skye to change her mind about going to Menno Simons.

The ironic thing about it, Angela thought as her mind drifted away from the speaker, was that although she was furthering her education on a music scholarship, she didn't plan to major in music. She was going into elementary ed. Skye, on the other hand, planned to pursue her music very seriously—just not through the educational system. She was going to the school of hard knocks—the world.

When the time finally came for the class members to stand and, one by one, hear their names called to receive a diploma, Angela did so with a flood of mixed emotions. It was exciting to be graduating and moving on. It was sad to think about the people she'd miss as their life journeys began to take them in different directions.

♫ ♫ ♫

The Blue Valley High School graduation that year was held on the last Saturday in May. Following the ceremonies, the graduates formed a line outside on the school lawn to greet and receive the well-wishes of friends and family members. A perfect spring Pennsylvania evening invited everyone to enjoy the occasion—an occasion that would continue in many of the graduates' homes as their parents hosted private parties for their son or daughter.

Angela stood between Skye and one of their best friends in the receiving line, shaking hands and receiving hugs, gifts, cards, and best wishes. Many of the well-wishers called her by name and told her how much they enjoyed her singing. Angela was used to the strong handshakes and loving hand-pats of men and women she didn't know. She received many that day, and some caught her attention more than others. But none caught and held her interest like the man at the end of the line.

From his clothes to his earrings and hairstyle, he didn't appear to be one of the "locals"—a fact he confirmed with his first words to Angela as he shook her hand. "I'm sorry—I don't know if you're Angela or Skye," he began. "My name's Jake Jordan. I'm here for my niece Carrie," he dropped her hand but continued talking. "Anyway, you girls are good. Real good. In fact, and I can't make any promises, but I'm pretty tight with an agent back in New York. I think I could persuade her to listen to you two."

Angela stared at the man with the long brown hair and hoop earrings. His face seemed as honest, open and friendly as the others that had just passed through the line. But while they had all congratulated her and wished her well, this guy ... this guy was offering an audition? In New York City?

She turned to Skye, who had sensed enough to move closer with curiosity. Then she looked at Jake again and said, "I'm Angela, and this is Skye. Skye, this is Jake Jordan."

"I'm pleased to meet you, Skye," Jake shook her hand. "Like I was telling Angela, you girls are something else. I'm thinking there's a pretty good chance I can get you two an audition with an agent I know in New York City."

It was Skye's turn to stare, but not for long. Within seconds she let out a loud whoop and hugged Angela, yelling "YES! YES! YES!" She let go of Angela, did a jumping dance in the grass, and then returned to Jake, who seemed quite amused by the commotion his words had caused. Skye looked him in the eyes and, her face suddenly serious, said, "You do mean that, don't you?"

This time Jake laughed as he tossed his hair back over his shoulder. "I said there's a pretty good chance. I'll see what I can do."

Skye's loud cries of joy had caught the attention of her parents and grandparents, who were visiting on the lawn. They strolled over to see what was going on.

"Mom and Dad, this guy from New York says he can get us an audition!" Skye was jumping again, and Angela noticed how obvious it was that she was wearing shorts under her robe. She wondered who else had caught on.

Jake turned to meet Ken and Becca, while Jonas and Sue Ann hung back. Angela stepped around the hyper Skye and approached her Amish grandparents. She knew they'd heard Skye's announcement, but she didn't know what they were thinking about it. The world of long-haired musicians and bands was certainly foreign to them, and one they viewed as full of worldly temptations and corruption. She'd expect them to be less than thrilled with this "opportunity."

"It's pretty exciting for Skye," Angela said to her grandparents. "It's what she's wanted to do for a long time, you know."

"And you? Will you go too?" Jonas asked, his eyes on Skye and Jake.

"To the audition? I don't know. But don't worry, I'll be at Menno Simons this fall. I want to be a teacher," Angela assured.

"I'm so glad to hear that," Sue Ann reached for her granddaughter's hand. "I've been looking forward to having you close by. I sure wish it was both of you, though."

"I know, Grandma, I know."

"Angela and Skye, collect your things and let's head home," Ken said abruptly. "I'm going to drive you girls in your car. I need to talk to you before we get home."

Her father's voice sounded very serious, and Angela wondered what in the world could be the matter. Was it Skye's clothes? Or something to do with the possible audition?

Whatever it was, it would take something pretty heavy to bring Skye down from her cloud nine, Angela figured. And why was it so important that they had to talk about it before the reception? A twitch of fear flipped through her stomach as Angela collected her cards and gifts.

"I'll go get the instruments and meet you at the car," she heard her father say.

ANGELA

THREE

ANGELA, SKYE, AND KEN got into the twins' car and left the Blue Valley High School parking lot. It wasn't very far to their home, and Angela wondered how soon her father would let them know why he had to drive them home and talk to them. She didn't have to wait long.

"I need to talk to you girls about something that happened at graduation," Ken began. "This is all so sudden, but we've also known it could happen at any time."

Angela, who was sitting in front with her father, looked at Skye in the back seat. The question marks in her mind were reflected in Skye's eyes.

"I don't know if either of you noticed a woman wearing dark glasses tonight," Ken continued, and Angela's heart jumped.

"I felt like she was watching me, and something made me suspicious that she might be Andrea, your mother. She said in her letter that she might show up sometime, and this would be a logical time."

Angela's heart was racing now. Their mother! She turned to look at Skye again, and the question marks had turned to shock.

"Our mother was there?" Skye exploded. "Are you sure?"

"I was suspicious enough to go up and talk to her. She didn't want to talk to me at first, but she finally did. Yes, it was her."

"What happened to her? Why didn't she come talk to us?" Skye was incredulous.

"She's very confused about whether or not you should meet each other. She wanted to see you so bad, but she didn't know how we'd feel about you meeting her."

"So what'd you tell her, Dad?" Skye was leaning forward in the back seat now.

"I told her she was welcome to come to the house tonight, or any other time, for that matter. She said she had to fly out early tomorrow morning, and she'd think about stopping by tonight."

"Do you think she will?" Angela found her voice.

"I have no idea, honey. Part of me says she will, and part of me remembers the scared teenager who didn't know how to face your birth eighteen years ago, and chose to leave the problem with somebody else. So I don't know, Angela, I don't know."

"She's gotta come see us!" Skye demanded. "She can't fly out here from *wherever* and then just leave again!"

"Where is she living, Dad?" Angela asked.

"In Florida."

"Is she married?"

"Yes."

"Does she have other children?"

"No."

Angela asked more questions about their biological mother, but Ken didn't have any more answers. Andrea had gotten more and more nervous the longer Ken talked to her, and had excused herself before he could find out very much about her. Angela could hear the emotion and frustration in Ken's voice as he related what had happened. This had to be hard for him too.

They had reached their split-level home in one of the housing developments outside of Blue Valley, and the street in front of their house was full of cars already. Angela wondered if her mother could possibly be there already. No, she wouldn't have walked into a house full of strangers.

"I told Becca about this, and she told Dawdis on the way home," Ken said, pulling into the driveway and activating the remote controlled garage door. "Let's just try to have a good time, and if she shows up, we'll deal with it then. If not, we'll live with that too. Okay?" He shut off the car and turned to Angela first, then Skye. "You going to be okay?"

They both nodded numbly. What else could they do, Angela wondered.

Inside, the house buzzed with friends and family members visiting with each other and eating finger foods. Angela felt disjointed and removed from the party being thrown for her and Skye. These people had no idea what was going through her heart right now.

Except for her mother and grandparents. While she smiled and greeted people along the way through the house, her eyes sought out the other people who knew. There, in the kitchen, Becca was busy replacing food on the plates, and her grandma was making punch. Angela made her way toward them and touched her mother on the shoulder. Their eyes met, and what Angela saw in her mother's disturbed her.

"You okay, Mom?" Angela said quietly.

"I hope so," Becca answered, the tension thick in her voice. She turned toward the counter and away from anyone who might hear. Angela stayed beside her. "It's just such bad timing," Becca continued. "Why tonight? Why not tomorrow, when it's just us here?"

Angela didn't know what to say. Her mother was right, but the angry edge in her voice surprised Angela. She hated this. A party that was supposed to be a highlight was turning sour fast.

The doorbell rang and Angela jumped. She felt her mother flinch beside her too. She heard the door open and her father greet someone, "Come in, come in, we were wondering if you'd make it."

Angela grabbed her mother's arm. Heart racing, she began walking out of the kitchen. Becca followed close behind. Where's Skye? Angela wondered.

They rounded the corner between the kitchen and living room to see Ken standing with the girls' music teacher, Mr. Toews. Angela smiled weakly in his direction. So, it was only Mr. Toews.

"Help yourself to some punch and food," Ken said to the latest arrival. "And ask the girls about the guy who talked to them after graduation —you'll want to hear about that!"

"Yeah, and ask the girls about their mother who *didn't* talk to them at graduation," Skye appeared at Angela's elbow, whispering the bitter words. Then, without skipping a beat, she followed Mr. Toews into the kitchen and began to tell him about Jake Jordan.

The evening dragged on. Every time the doorbell ran, Angela's insides churned. She couldn't eat a bite of food, and just sipped punch to keep her dry mouth moistened. Skye and Ken were maintaining the facade quite well, but Angela was having a hard time with the small talk and telling people about her college plans. Becca wasn't herself at all. Jonas and Sue Ann visited pleasantly with anyone who sought them out, but Angela knew they felt the tension too. She found herself checking the cuckoo clock a lot. The thirty minutes between the bird's hour and half-hour appearances felt like forever.

The cuckoo was singing eleven times when Angela dropped onto the couch, exhausted. The last guest had left a few minutes ago. The rest of the family, including Jonas and Sue Ann, looked as emotionally fried as Angela felt. Even Ken and Skye let the facade drop. What an evening. And Andrea never showed up.

"I just want to know why you invited her here tonight," Becca said, collapsing onto the couch beside Angela and staring at Ken who was leaning against the front door. He hadn't moved since he said goodnight to the last person.

"It seemed like the right thing to do at the time," Ken said, his voice low and tired. "And I still think it was. She's their mother. She has the right to see them."

"And what about our rights?" Becca retorted. "Don't we have a right to celebrate their graduation without the possible *first-time* appearance of Andrea threatening to ruin it all?"

Angela shivered. Her parents rarely argued. She hated to hear this.

"I'm sorry, but I'm tired," Becca's words apologized, but her voice still stung. "Mom and I worked hard getting food and stuff ready for this party, plus we're really busy at the rides. I'm physically and emotionally strung out right now. I just wasn't ready for this tonight."

"And then she doesn't show up anyhow," Skye added. "I knew she wouldn't."

Jonas leaned forward in the rocking chair he was sitting in and stroked his long white beard thoughtfully. Angela watched him. She wondered what he and Grandma thought of this whole mess.

"When your mother left you girls here, she was trying to do the best for you," he said, the words coming out slowly, as if he were thinking about each one individually. "It was the best she knew to do at the time. Tonight she was at your graduation. Ken saw her. He talked to her. He invited her here. It was what he felt was right to do."

Jonas paused before he continued. "I don't know if you are all upset that she didn't come, or would be more upset if she had. The thing is, she didn't. What's behind us is behind us. Let's all go to bed and see what tomorrow brings. One day at a time." Jonas stood up and made his way toward Sue Ann, who was next to Becca on the couch. "And I'd like to take this fine woman to my room with me," he reached his hand out to Sue Ann.

The family laughed lightly. It had only been a few hours, but Angela felt like she hadn't laughed for days. It felt good. What a wise and wonderful man her Dawdi was.

♫ ♫ ♫

AS TIRED AS THEY WERE, Angela and Skye talked long after the lights were out in their room that night. Skye's bitterness was mellowing a bit, and more and more yearning came through her voice as she talked about their mother. Maybe they should look for her, she said, now that they at least knew which state she lived in. Angela agreed that might be something to pursue.

They talked about Jake Jordan and the audition. He'd said he'd call within a few weeks.

"If he calls, will you go to the audition with me?" Skye asked.

"I'd go along, but not to sing with you. You can do it by yourself," Angela assured.

"I don't know."

"Of course you can. This is your dream. You can! No problem."

"Maybe I'll get into a band that'll come to Kansas," Skye giggled. "Then you can come to the concert and I'll invite you on stage to sing 'You're My Sister' with me."

"That'd be cool," Angela smiled in the darkness.

"I bet you'll find a guy at Menno Simons," Skye teased. "Some farmer who needs a perfect little wife to take care of the house and children."

"That wouldn't be so bad. We'll see. I really want to teach."

"I don't see how you can think about teaching children all day long. They would drive me crazy. Always asking questions, always hanging on you, always begging for something."

"But they're so sweet," Angela argued. "And so open to learning."

"Yeah, if they sit still long enough to learn."

"They do, and learning isn't always a sitting still activity."

"Okay, okay, Ms. Martin," Skye giggled. "Ms. Martin, Ms. Martin, can I go to the bathroom? Please? I gotta go right now!"

Angela laughed, "Yes, Skye, you may go. And remember to wash your hands before you come back."

Skye got out of her bed and left the room, still chuckling. A memory and an idea flashed through Angela's mind. Turning on her bedside light, she saw the package of gummy worms where Skye had left them on her desk. Jumping out of bed, Angela hurried to the desk, grabbed the bag, and poured the worms onto Skye's mattress. Then she turned off the light and quickly slipped back into bed.

Skye returned soon and was in her bed only seconds when her screams sent giggles convulsing through Angela. Skye couldn't get her light turned on fast enough to see what she'd been lying on, and when she did, she picked up a handful of worms and flung them at Angela.

"Hey, I thought you liked them," Angela broke into a new round of girlish laughter, as a gummy worm war broke out in the upstairs bedroom of the Martin house.

ANGELA

FOUR

THE DOORBELL RANG on a ranch-style farmhouse in central Iowa. Angela Swartzendruber left the photo albums open on the oak dining room table where she'd been looking at them. The reporter would probably want to see them—she'd said on the phone she wanted to talk about her and Skye and how their lives were so different even though they were identical twins.

Angela opened the door and greeted the woman in her twenties with city-short hair. You could always tell women with city hair cuts, Angela thought—they had style and "that look" to them. This reporter had come all the way from New York—something Angela still found hard to believe.

"Hello, Angela, I'm Karin Keeston."

"Hi, Karin, come in." Angela stood back from the door.

"Thank you. I appreciate you taking time for this interview today," Karin said, following Angela to the living room.

"I think we'll sit here at the table where we can look at the pictures if you want to." Angela indicated a chair at the table in front of a large bay window.

"Sounds good to me." Karin sat down, placing a large poster, notepad, camera, and tape recorder on the table. Angela noticed the bright poster immediately, and recognized her sister Skye.

"Quite a picture of Skye you've got there," she said, her eyes taking in the woman who looked so much like her and yet so foreign. Skye's eyes bothered her. Was it the make-up that made them look so hard, so haunted, so unsettled? Or was it the soul within her that glared through the green eyes and dared the viewer to look away?

"It's hot off the press," Karin said. "They're using it for the next tour. Skye's the opening act for High Five and she's getting some good publicity. She's a very talented performer."

"Yes, she is," Angela agreed. "Can I get you something to drink while we talk?"

"Maybe later," Karin said. "Do you mind if I tape our conversation?"

"No, that's fine."

"Well, like I said when I called you, we want to do a story that features you and Skye and how it happens that, as identical twins, one of you is an up-and-coming rock star and you are living a quiet life here in the middle of Iowa," Karin began. "Have you two always been so different?"

"Yes, and no," Angela said thoughtfully. "It wasn't as obvious as children, maybe, but definitely by the time we graduated from high school we knew we would be heading in separate directions. Skye wanted to get into the music business, and I wanted to go to college to get an elementary ed degree."

"And that's what happened?"

"Yes, pretty much."

"How did Skye get her start in the music industry?"

"We performed together a lot when we were growing up, and we did a song that Skye wrote at our high school graduation. A guy was there who knew an agent in New York, and she offered us an audition."

"Both of you?"

"Yes. I went along to New York, but I didn't sing with her. We both knew she needed to do this alone because I was going on to college."

"And you couldn't be tempted by an audition and possible opportunity to make it big time?"

"Not really," Angela's eyes scanned the farmyard scene outside her window. She could see her husband Jon walking between the hog buildings, and behind them, tall corn stretched into the distance under the summer haze.

Karin's eyes followed Angela's. "Or did you know you'd meet the perfect guy at college and he'd take you away to this peaceful country home?" she said, half-teasing.

"No, I didn't know, but I had a feeling everything would work out, and it has so far," Angela said. "I did meet Jon at Menno Simons College, and I've been able to teach here in Elm City for four years. I love teaching children. But," Angela paused and smiled at Karin, "I'm just going to substitute teach this fall because we're expecting our first child in January, and I plan to stay home after that."

"Wow! Congratulations!" Karin leaned back in her chair. She looked at Angela, and then down at the poster of Skye. "What blows me away is how completely opposite each other you seem to be! Did you get these different traits from your parents? Tell me about them."

The question hit Angela cold. She hadn't even thought about it coming up. The issue of their adoption was not a secret among family and friends. But the media? The media could have a heyday with this one. Especially since they didn't know who their biological father was, and had never talked to their mother. She could just see the media trying to locate her parents, especially with Skye being such an up-and-coming star. Oh no, she thought. She couldn't talk about it. Not without checking with Skye first.

Karin was talking again, and Angela heard the curiosity in her voice. "Angela? Your parents?"

"Karin, there are some things I'm not able to talk about right now, and I hope you'll understand," Angela said quietly. "What I can tell you is that both Skye and I seemed to have unusually good musical abilities from the time we were small, and our parents helped us to cultivate those."

Angela could see the questions flooding across Karin's face. Karin knew she'd tapped something and it was going to drive her crazy not to get to the bottom of it. Angela knew that's what reporters did, and she just prayed that this one wouldn't get rude. She didn't want to be pushed.

"Are your parents musicians?" Karin asked.

"No. They own several businesses in Gary County, Pennsylvania."

"Gary County! That's where a lot of Amish live! Are your parents Amish?" Karin asked, and from the look on her face, Angela could tell that Karin thought she'd uncovered the secret. "Rock Star Grew Up Amish"—Angela could see the headlines now. But that wasn't the truth.

"No they aren't," Angela said. "I'm sorry, Karin, but let's stay with what you indicated this interview would be about."

"That's fine," Karin said, and a slight edge had crept into her voice. "Tell me about yourself then. You went to—which college did you say that was?"

"Menno Simons in Kansas. A private Mennonite school. I graduated four years ago with an elementary education degree, married Jon Swartzendruber, and we've lived here on his parents' farm since they retired two years ago. I taught first grade for four years at Elm City. We're active in Elm City Mennonite Church, and I direct the children's choir there, plus sing in a quartet. I'm very happy here and feel like I'm exactly where God wants me to be."

"Say more about that."

"About what?"

"About being where God wants you to be."

"I believe that each of us, as children of God, are called to certain areas or ministries while we're here on earth, and we're given skills and abilities to use in those areas. I believe God gave me a wonderful husband to walk alongside and to share life together, and I pray we'll also have a family. That's one place I believe God wants me to be—with my husband and children. I also believe that I owe it to God to use my musical abilities where I can, and I'm trying to do that."

"Do you think Skye was called to be a rock artist?"

"I can't answer for Skye," Angela said, her eyes finding the poster again.

"But what do you think?"

"I think you will have to interview her for her story, and me for mine," Angela said firmly. "Do you want to look at any of the pictures?"

"Sure, and I'll take that drink now too," Karin said, turning to the photo album.

Angela was glad for the excuse to get up and go into the kitchen. She'd been feeling a little queasy, and she didn't know if it was nerves or the baby or both. Anyway, the break felt good.

She returned a few minutes later with tall glasses of iced tea, and Jon beside her. He'd come into the house while she was pouring the tea, and she figured it'd be good for him to meet Karin, and vice versa. After all, he was a big part of her life, and Karin wanted to know about her life.

"Jon Swartzendruber," he said, holding out a strong brown hand. "Pleased to meet you."

"The pleasure is mine," Karin returned, and Angela could see Karin's eyes take in her good-looking husband. Jon stood six feet, one inch, and as solid as long days on the farm could make a man. In the summer, he wore denim shirts with the sleeves cut out, and his muscled arms turned bronze. His close-cropped brown hair curled as much as it could, and his brown eyes were as honest and deep as the Iowa soil he knew so well. "A dying breed" some people called these sons who wanted to stay on the family farm, but there wasn't anything dying about this young man. He rippled with quiet, confident energy and strength.

"Jon could take you out in the tractor to see some of the farm if that interests you," Angela said, then seeing Karin's brow wrinkle, added, "It has a cab and air conditioning."

Karin's expression changed immediately. "I'd love to! And can we stop to take some pictures?"

"Sure. I'll even try to stay upwind of the hog barns," Jon chuckled. "But since it's Angela's favorite part of the farm, maybe you can get some pictures of her in there later."

"Or maybe her film will be full before we have that 'opportunity,'" Angela joked back.

Karin took her glass of tea and left with Jon for their short tour of the farm and some nearby fields. Angela stood by the table, sipping her tea and staring at the poster. Sometimes it was hard to believe they were twin sisters. And at the same time, she felt a deep commonality with Skye. It was hard to explain, but she felt that somehow she knew and understood Skye's heart and soul much more than Skye understood Angela. Or herself, for that matter. Maybe Skye just didn't take the time to try to understand the deepest yearnings of her soul, and she certainly didn't have much time for her boring sister. She was too busy succeeding, making it big in the music world, going for the gusto. And all the while, Angela mused, what Skye really wanted and needed was people who loved her, a place to call home, an avenue to sing where her skills were appreciated.

She probably thinks she has that, Angela realized. Skye had fans adoring her for her music. They loved her, in a sense. The people she traveled with had become her family, and of course she still had Angela, their parents and grandparents. She was on the road too much to have a real home, but she said she loved that lifestyle.

Skye probably didn't know she wasn't happy, but Angela could see it in her eyes on that poster. The reporter's question haunted Angela. "Do you think Skye was called to be a rock artist?"

She knew how Skye would answer that question. She'd toss her long blonde hair behind her and give that can't-resist-it grin and she'd say, "Called? That stage has been callin' me since I was a child! You bet your acres of corn I was called!"

Angela smiled to herself. She hadn't seen her sister for months, but she could hear her talking as if they'd never been apart. Although their lives had changed a lot in the eight years since they left high school and took different roads, the bond that had created them as twins could never be severed.

SKYE

SKYE

ONE

THE E-MAIL FROM HER FANS flooded the computer screen, and Skye smiled as she clicked through the messages. She shifted positions in her cramped living quarters of the bus and reached for her mug of coffee. Yes, they loved her. She loved it that they loved her.

But then it was time. She'd paid her dues. After ten years in back-up bands and singing groups, she'd finally been given the chance to open for a band. All by herself. And after a few years of that, the sales of her CD's were good enough to give her the headline show. Now, at 33, she had her own band, her own bus, and she was rolling. She was used to people standing in line, hoping for her autograph. She was used to being recognized on the street, pointed at, and whispered about. She loved it. She liked being a star.

The e-mail messages all started to look the same, and then she caught a different one. Oh yes, today was Sunday. Her sister Angela always e-mailed her on Sunday. And there it was, as dependable as … well, as dependable as Angela always had been. Skye swallowed the dark black liquid in her mug as her eyes scanned the screen.

Dear Skye: It's a gorgeous spring morning here in Iowa, but it looks like it'll be one of those sticky humid days again. I got up early this morning to have some quiet time before it's time to wake the boys and get them ready for church. Plus I wanted to spend a few more minutes with my Sunday school lesson. Anyway, I'm done with that now and had some extra time and thought I'd write you. I wonder where you are and how you're doing today—I'll be looking forward to hearing back from you. Here, I'm keeping busy with the garden, the boys, and helping Jon whenever he needs it.

The other day I had to go to town to get some parts for the tractor, and the pickup had a flat on the way in. So there I was with boys who are 2, 5, and 7, and they are going to "help Mom change the tire." Now I'm not a totally helpless woman, but when it comes to changing a tire along the side of the road with three "helpful" little boys who could get hurt—well I'd rather have some help. And you know what? Cars kept driving by. Maybe they were in a hurry to get someplace. Or maybe they couldn't see the flat—it was on the ditch side—and thought I was just stopping for the boys to take a potty break. I don't know, but it was hard to believe. Then along came this spanking white Cadillac. I knew it wouldn't stop. But it slowed down, and it did stop. A businessman rolled down the electric window and asked me if I was having problems. I said we had a flat. He got out of his car and this man had expensive clothes on—I mean expensive. I suggested we could call someone on his cell phone, although I knew Jon wouldn't be reachable. The man said no, he'd just help me change the tire. And he did. When we were done, his clothes were dirty and wet with sweat 'cause it was a hot day. I couldn't believe it! I asked him what I owed him and he gave me ten dollars and told me to buy cold drinks and ice cream for the boys and myself when we got to town.

I guess that doesn't sound very exciting compared to your life, but it was an interesting experience for me and the boys. We talked about it all the way to town, and it'll be awhile before they forget "the fancy man who changed our tire."

This week the boys are taking swimming lessons, so

that'll keep us busy in the mornings. Well, I've gotta get going now. Take care of yourself, sis!

Love you,
Angela

Skye sat back and pulled the bus curtain aside. The countryside of—which state where they in? Missouri, that's right—swept past her window. How different their lives had turned out—her and her twin sister. Angela was so happy being married, raising children, teaching Sunday school, and her idea of a good story was being helped by a rich man when she had a flat tire. Good for her, Skye thought. Maybe they'd drop in on Angela's family sometime when they were in the area—the band would probably get off on the peaceful country atmosphere—at least for an afternoon and evening. But she'd surely die of boredom if they stayed much longer.

She needed the music. She needed the pulsing, driving, pushing beat of the band behind her, and the microphone in her hand. She needed to kiss the mic with her words and her mouth, and send the songs out to the screaming crowds. She needed to hear their clapping and their cheers begging for more, and she needed to give them more.

In fact, she'd been thinking about that. Her latest idea involved a Harley. She wanted to ride a rumbling Harley-Davidson motorcycle onto the stage. She had a song brewing in her mind too—a riding a Harley song. She needed to talk to Max about it—he'd come up with the right sound. And they needed to start looking at Harleys.

♫ ♫ ♫

ANOTHER CITY, another concert. Skye stood backstage that evening, her skin-tight black jeans molding her slender frame. The low-cut, shimmery silver blouse ended at her midriff, and tucked into one of the jean loops at the waist was a faded red bandanna.

Call it superstitious, call it sentimental, she wasn't sure. Years ago, when she was 18 and going to New York for her first audition, she'd taken the bandanna along—the one her Amish grandfather had given her as a child. She'd figured she might need it to cry in if she got turned down. But she'd been given a part in a back-up group for a band playing the clubs in New York, and she'd kept the bandanna with her ever since. She found different ways to use it—around her neck, to tie her long hair back, around her waist or ankle. Sometimes she hung it from her guitar. It was just a part of her scene, and people came to expect it. In fact, there was some talk about selling replicas at the souvenir stands. Why not, she figured. It should work. Skye fingered the bandanna at her side. Amazing what you could sell fans and make money.

The opening act was over, and her band nearly set up. One of her assistants brought her a mug, and Skye took a sip. And then she remembered … she'd taken her insulin shot but hadn't had anything to eat since then.

"Dusty! Quick!" she hailed the assistant. "Run back to the dressing room and bring me something to eat real quick!"

Stupid, she told herself. Stupid, stupid, stupid. Just what you need to do—get shaky on stage. You are so stupid!

Dusty returned, out of breath, and handed Skye a banana and some cheese and crackers. She shoved them into her mouth as fast as she could chew, chasing the food with sips from the mug. "Thanks, babe," she said to Dusty. "You saved my life."

The band stood poised to run onto the stage as the announcer began the intro. Skye took another swig from the mug, gave her band the thumbs up sign, and they ran up to take their places. Skye followed as the spotlights swept the center stage and caught her in the middle, her blouse shimmering blue, then green, then purple. She grabbed the mic as the crowd welcomed her, and broke into a pounding auditorium-shaking hard rock song. She'd done this song hundreds of times, and she still loved it.

The song over, Skye stood and absorbed the applause around her. Then as it faded away, she addressed the crowd.

"I'm going to do this song now, because I do it at every concert. But it's kinda mellow, and after this one, we're going to get cra-zee, if you know what I mean!" The crowd yelled and cheered, and Skye bowed her head until the noise died down. "The name of the song is 'You're My Sister,' and Angela, my sister, this one's for you!"

The soft strains of the song filled the auditorium, and it felt to Skye as if 10,000 people were holding their breath. She sang from her heart, as she did every time. Yes, part of it was the performer in her. She knew how to milk the crowd. But part of her was eighteen again, singing with Angela on the Blue Valley High School stage. And the truth was, now that they didn't see each other very often, her most emotional contact with her twin was when she sang their song.

As the last strains of the violin trembled into closure, the audience erupted. Skye stood with her head down, then brought it up again and bowed. "Thank you," she said. "Thank you."

♫ ♫ ♫

"YOU WERE HOT, girl, really hot," Max, the bass guitarist, cuffed Skye lightly on the chin as he slumped down beside her in the bus after the concert. "You had them eatin' out of your hand."

"Yeah, who'd have believed down here in hicksville Missouri they'd even heard of rock," Skye smiled, trying to ignore the crushing fatigue settling through her body. She'd noticed it several other times—a tiredness that seemed more than her usual after-concert exhaustion. A nurse had told her it could be her kidneys, and suggested Skye see a doctor. But she had concerts to do, and no time to be sick. So Skye was putting up with it. She just slept more than she had before.

"I'm crashing," she stood up slowly, turning to Max. "Hey, do me a favor. Be thinkin' about what you can do with that bass of yours that sounds like a Harley. I'm gonna get me one and ride it on stage one of these times, and we need a song to go with it. What'dya think?"

"I think you'll not only have them eating out of your hand, you'll have them *drooling*," Max enthused. "But you gotta let me drive it."

"No problem. But first we gotta find one."

"I'll be lookin,'" Max promised. "'Cause I gotta hear one to be able to write the song."

"Right," Skye said. "Later."

"Later."

Skye pushed the curtain aside that separated her private quarters from the bands' bunks, and fell into the bed. She was dead. A bone-weary, total exhaustion. She was going to have to see about getting uppers to get some energy back.

Soon after Skye flipped on the small TV mounted above the bed, she fell asleep. The bus rolled on through the night, leaving Missouri, weaving its way through the Arkansas hills.

SKYE

TWO

THE BODY-NUMBING FATIGUE was getting worse. Worse, and more often. Skye was getting through concerts by popping uppers. She made it through the next concert in Oklahoma but collapsed in the bus immediately afterwards. She didn't even hang around to sign autographs, and that was very unlike Skye. She hated the idea of going to a doctor, but she was beginning to think she'd have to. She promised herself she would, after the concert in Vicksburg, Kansas.

When it came to lifestyle, Skye had removed herself about as far as she could go from her Amish grandparents in Kansas. Nearly everything she was and did bordered on an insult to their culture and traditions. From her appearance to her songs, from her life on the road to her lack of commitment to a church, she epitomized some of the worst of what "the world" offered. Even so, she carried fond memories with her of her childhood summers in Kansas, and she decided to stop and see her grandparents while the band was in Vicksburg. They weren't far from the city, and it wouldn't take long to run over to see them.

She didn't want to take the whole bus, and that's when the idea hit. If they could find a Harley in Vicksburg, she'd just ride it out to Wellsford to visit Dawdis! That would blow their minds for sure—their granddaughter showing up on a big bike. She hoped she'd feel up to it. She would.

The bus pulled into Vicksburg late evening on the first Friday in June. The concert was Saturday evening. That morning, Skye woke up feeling better than she had in a long time. Maybe drinking more water and less alcohol was helping . Maybe she could get by for a while without seeing a doctor after all.

The band gorged themselves at a breakfast buffet, and then stopped at a Harley-Davidson store Max located in the yellow pages. Skye could hardly wait to look at the bikes. The more she thought about it, the more she wanted one. Now.

A guy about Skye's age met them at the door when the whole band strode toward the shop. Tall, slender, wearing a long black ponytail, he fit the stereotype of a Harley owner. Black t-shirt, black jeans, black boots. The sides of his eyes crinkled when he smiled, and he was smiling at Skye. She smiled back and stuck out her hand.

"Skye," she said by way of introduction. His handshake felt good. Strong.

"Bo," he returned. "Bo Riggs."

Skye's heart thudded. She had never heard a voice quite like that one. To say it was low wasn't enough. To say it was sexy was maybe too much. After all, he'd only said his name. She wanted to hear that voice some more.

"We thought we might buy a Harley today," Skye said, her eyes sweeping the store and settling back on Bo. "You got any for sale?"

"Yes, and no," his deep voice answered from beside her. "Harley's are in demand, you know. Mostly we sell used ones—and they go out fast—and new ones by order only."

"Order only?" Skye asked. "You mean a person can't buy a new bike today?"

Bo chuckled, and it sounded like a soft rumble in this throat. "Oh you can *buy* one today, Skye, you just can't *have* it today. We'll take your money anytime." Skye could hear the rest of the band enjoying that comment from their different places in the shop. Max had already found a bike to sit on.

Skye smiled at Bo. "And if I write you a check today, how soon do I get my Harley?'

"It could be up to two years."

"Two years!"

"That's the waiting list right now."

Skye walked up to a shiny black bike. Slipping one blue-jeaned leg over the seat, she settled onto the soft padding and rested her arms on the bars in front of her.

"This is a demo," Bo stood beside her. "You're looking at over fifteen grand for this one."

Fifteen thousand dollars for a motorcycle. Skye's smile spread across her face and wouldn't quit. The crazy thing about this was that she could even afford to think about it. A few years ago, she could dream but that was all. Now she could start making some of those dreams happen. If she wanted a Harley, she could actually buy one. Except that she'd have to wait two years. She hated to wait.

"I was wanting to go visit my grandparents in Wellsford this morning on a Harley," she half-pouted in Bo's direction. "Plus I want to drive one on stage at one of my next concerts," she paused. "This waiting business doesn't work for me at all."

"I can understand that," Bo leaned against the counter and studied Skye. She felt his gaze, and returned it. For the first time, she noticed his eyes. Slate blue.

"I'd be glad to take you to your grandparents on my bike," he finally said matter-of-factly. "Maybe give you a few driving lessons along the way."

"Really?" It never occurred to Skye to hesitate. "When?"

"Now's as good as any time. I'll just close the shop until we get back."

"That would be so cool," Skye bubbled. "You know I'll owe you one."

"You buy a bike from me, and we'll be even," Bo laughed his low deep laugh.

Bo motioned Skye to follow him to the back of his shop, where his Harley was parked. He pushed it out the wide door, and Skye couldn't help but notice his body as he threw a leg over the bike and gave it a hard kick-start. The bike roared to life, and

Skye felt a surge of her own go through her. What was it about this man? She'd been around many men in her career, and now she was feeling like a 16-year-old again on a first date. She looked at Bo's left hand. No ring.

The hour-long drive to Wellsford passed entirely too fast for Skye. She certainly didn't mind sitting close behind Bo, and it was incredibly refreshing to watch the Kansas scenery pass so close at hand. She knew she really wasn't any closer than being in the bus, but oh what a different feeling! The bus was big and cumbersome and protected her from the outdoors. Being on a motorcycle put her into the outdoors. She felt like she could almost touch and smell the ripening wheat in the fields they passed, and it brought back wonderful memories of her times in Kansas as a girl.

Bo slowed down as they approached the Amish community of Wellsford, and Skye leaned forward until her face was near his.

"Did I tell you my grandparents are Amish?"

Bo laughed lightly. "I'd say you're kidding except that I know there are a lot of them here in Wellsford. You probably aren't kidding."

"Nope. Not at all."

"Does that mean we don't offer your grandpa a ride?"

It was Skye's turn to giggle.

"We could try. But not only is he Amish, he's a minister, so I'm not sure he'd take us up on it."

It had been several years since Skye had seen her grandparents, Jonas and Sue Ann Bontrager, but she heard about them through her mother and sister. Jonas was 78 and Sue Ann 80, but they still lived on their farm in a "Dawdi-house" and were in quite good health. Their youngest daughter Emma lived in the larger farmhouse with her family—following the Amish tradition of the youngest daughter living on her parents' farm and taking care of them in their senior years.

Bo rumbled the Harley into the farmyard that Skye remembered so well, and rolled to a stop next to a huge cottonwood tree. Skye noticed a number of barefoot Amish children scamper toward the house and the screen door slammed behind them. Just as quickly, the screen door filled with curious little faces. Emma's kids, Skye smiled. How many did she have anyway?

Soon Emma's white-capped face topped the younger ones in the door, and Skye waved. She saw the surprise on Emma's face and then the door swung open. Barefoot, Emma walked out onto the porch and down the wooden steps.

"Skye?" she said. "What in the world?"

"Hi, Emma!" Skye was off the cycle and running toward her. "It's good to see you!"

The women embraced, and by that time they were surrounded by curious children. Skye turned to them, and then she heard her name again.

"Skye? Is that you?"

A slightly bent, white-haired Amish man was making his way across the yard, and Skye left Emma's porch to meet him.

"Dawdi!" she cried out. "How are you?"

The rock star and Amish minister embraced for a long time, and Skye couldn't believe the wetness in her eyes when they separated. She looked into the blue eyes of her grandfather Jonas and said, "Oh Dawdi, it's good to see you!"

"And it's good to see you too, my granddaughter," Jonas replied. "It's been a long time."

"I know, too long." Now that she was here, it really felt like it had been too long. "Where's Grandma?"

"Oh, she's at one of those hen parties," Jonas said. "You know, where the women all go to quilt and gossip."

Skye laughed. "And what do the men do?'

"We go to coffee," Jonas replied. "But of course we men just discuss things, we don't gossip." His blue eyes teased just like Skye remembered.

"Do you want to come in? You and your friend?" Jonas asked, nodding toward Bo, who was still sitting on the bike.

"Oh, he's not really my friend, he just brought me out here," Skye said, and realized that sounded strange. The expression on Jonas's face confirmed her thoughts.

"What I mean is, I didn't want to have the whole bus come out here, and I'm thinking about buying a motorcycle, so we went to a shop today to look at them. But a person can't buy one without ordering it, so the shop owner offered to bring me out here," Skye didn't know if that explanation helped things or not.

"Well, does he have a name and does he want to come in?" Jonas seemed to take it all in stride.

"Bo! You wanna come inside?" Skye called.

"You can all come over here," Emma called from her porch, where she still stood with her cluster of children. "I have fresh chocolate chip cookies."

"I'm in," Bo said, swinging his leg over the seat and walking toward Emma's house. He stopped when he met Skye and Jonas on their way over as well. "Sir, my name's Bo Riggs," he said, extending his hand. "I'm pleased to meet you."

"Jonas Bontrager," Jonas said, taking the firm handshake. "Quite a buggy you've got there," he nodded in the direction of the shiny black Harley.

Bo chuckled and Skye thought her face would crack from smiling. How could she have forgotten what a likable, easy-going man her grandfather was? And Bo—he seemed completely at ease among these people whose dress and lifestyle made them seem so different.

Jonas and Bo were talking as they walked toward the house, and Skye caught her grandfather's words "Reminds me of a black horse I owned once," and the next thing she knew Bo was listening intently to Jonas tell about a horse named Preacher and she figured she might as well turn her attention to Emma and the children.

At that moment, her evening concert was the farthest thing from her mind.

SKYE

THREE

THE TIME WITH HER GRANDFATHER, Emma, and Emma's children passed entirely too fast for Skye. Bo warmed his way into the hearts of her relatives, and before she knew what was happening, Bo had offered to take the children on short motorcycle rides and Emma had said it was okay. Blew Skye away, it did. But it reminded her of something she'd known years ago yet forgotten as more distance had grown between her and her Amish relatives—that they were regular people clothed in a conservative lifestyle. The kids had a blast on the cycle, and Skye had a feeling Emma and maybe even Dawdi would have succumbed to its lure if they'd known no one in the community would see them.

By mid-afternoon Skye knew they had to get back to Vicksburg to get ready for the concert and regretfully tore herself away from the comfortable peace of the Bontrager farmstead. She slid onto the seat of the Harley behind Bo, and this time the children weren't running and hiding. They, along with their mother and grandfather, were standing in a smiling circle around the big black bike. Bo and Skye said their goodbyes and waved as they rolled out the lane and onto the road.

The trip back to Vicksburg gave Skye time to reflect on what had happened so far that day, and three things kept capturing her attention. First, she'd loved being with her relatives. Second, Bo was a wonderful guy. Third, she was starting to feel very tired.

Maybe it was the ride, sitting close to Bo. Maybe it was a fear of the future she couldn't define. Maybe it was just another wild Skye idea. Whatever lay behind the request, before she said good-bye to Bo that afternoon, Skye asked him if he'd be willing to drive her on stage that evening on his Harley. He grinned that slow grin of his and rumbled in his deep voice that he'd have to think about it. When Skye's face began to fall in disappointment, Bo added that he'd thought about it already and he probably could do that for her. They agreed to meet in two hours to see how to pull it off in the Vicksburg arena.

♫ ♫ ♫

A LITTLE BIT OF NERVOUSNESS was good. It kept her sharp. But that evening, Skye found herself more than a little nervous. And she knew why. The Harley ride, and the nagging fatigue. One had her psyched and hyper. The other scared her to death. What if she couldn't finish the concert? What if she collapsed on stage? Horrors.

But she couldn't think about it. She'd taken her uppers, and they'd have to get her through one more concert. That, and the adrenalin. Good ole Max had quickly fine-tuned the "Harley song" he'd been working on, and the band had done some last minute jamming. They were as ready as they could be.

Skye, Bo, and the band's manager stood next to the Harley in the roped off section behind the arena stage. The red bandanna hugged Skye's little waist that evening. She adjusted it, watching as Bo's slender hips slid onto the bike seat. Man, he looked good tonight. Skye followed him onto the seat, and her arms encircled his waist. Unnecessary, she knew, but somehow she needed to do it. Bo turned his head toward her and his voice added chills to her edgy nerves. "This ride's for you, Skye."

Her arms tightened around his waist. Bo, the Harley, the pre-concert rush of adrenalin, the pills—Skye was flying now. The rumble of Max's bass guitar roared through the PA system, as the announcer built up the crowd. "And now, ladies and gentlemen, please welcome to Vicksburg—on a Harley from our own

Vicksburg Harley-Davidson shop—the one, the only … SKYE!"

The band exploded into the new song, and Bo's bike surged beneath her. A rush of adrenaline pushed through Skye, and then they were in the arena. The noise of the band, the bike, the crowd was deafening. The bike flew down the aisle lined with security people and Skye could feel the energy of the people packed around them. A huge building full of fans who were there for her! Screaming, clapping, whistling—all for her! Skye's heart seemed desperate to escape from her chest. What a rush! Her hands flew to her waist in a spontaneous action, and she untied the bandanna. Lifting it high in her fist, she rode the Harley through the spotlights sweeping the arena in crazy circles. Yes, Yes, YES!

The Harley crested the ramp and Bo made a sharp right turn onto the stage. The lights glistened off the bike's shiny black body as they cruised the circumference of the stage, and the crowd went crazy. "SKYE! SKYE! SKYE!" The chant rose up and took over. Within moments the arena shook with her name and Skye was high. High on praise and power.

They circled the stage once, and then Skye jumped lightly off the back of the bike. Impulsively, she gave Bo an unrehearsed peck on the cheek, and the crowd erupted in response. Some of them knew the owner of the local Harley shop, others just loved the moment. Skye took the mic waiting for her on a stand.

"Hello Vicksburg!" she crooned. "How'd you like that Harley? How about a hand for my friend Bo Riggs?"

The audience answered with cheers as Bo waved and rolled down the ramp and aisle. Then they turned their attention back to Skye.

"Tonight I'm going to do something I've never done before," Skye said, and the crowd fell quiet. "Well, actually, two things," she added. "The Harley was the first one." The crowd cheered again, but not for long. They seemed eager to hear what was coming next.

"I'm going to tell you the story behind the bandanna," Skye continued. "Most of you know that about an hour from here, there's an Amish community called Wellsford. Well, that's where my grandparents live. They're Amish. And as a kid, my twin sister and I would spend two weeks every summer with them. One summer, I was upset about something, and my grandfather—Dawdi we call him—gave me this bandanna to cry into. He told me to keep it for the future, whenever I might need to cry. I've had it with me ever since." Skye fingered the bandanna and realized how incredibly quiet the arena had become. In a matter of seconds, the loud crowd was so still, she could hear someone coughing high up in the stands.

"This afternoon I went to visit my grandfather and other family members," Skye said. "I realized what wonderful people they are, and how important family is. The first song I'm going to do tonight is for the closest family member I have—my twin sister." The band picked up the cue and began the intro. "Angela, this one's for you," Skye said, and the crowd broke into applause.

I look into the mirror and I see you,
Sometimes I know how you will feel even before you do,
We're two of a kind and yet we're different in so many ways,
And I am proud to say you're my sister.

Skye finished the first verse, and moved into the chorus.

With God on our side, we made it, you and I,
And we wouldn't change a thing
for all the stars in the sky;
And if tomorrow comes too fast,
Make each moment last today,
And the good Lord will remain to lead the way.

The tremor coming through the words as she sang surprised Skye, and she realized that she was missing Angela. She hadn't felt that for a long time. The third verse flowed out of her heart and over the quiet audience.

We'll beat the odds again, I'm sure.
I hope this world gives you everything you want and more;
We're separate lives here on earth,
But two hearts joined together at birth,
And you can have my shoulder, sister, when you hurt.

Skye felt an overwhelming urge to see Angela as she repeated the chorus—an urge she couldn't explain or put away. She'd make time to do that real soon, she promised herself, bowing as the applause washed over her at the end of the song. Yes, she'd make time to go see Angela real soon.

♫ ♫ ♫

THE UPPERS, and sheer adrenalin carried Skye for over an hour of her hard-driving, throbbing rock songs, but three-fourths of the way through her usual two-hour concert, Skye knew she wasn't going to make it. A body-breaking fatigue was suddenly taking over. Not only that, but she was having trouble remembering some words. It scared her. It scared her bad.

She managed to cue the band to do the two songs they usually ended with, and prayed the band manager would cue the lights gal. The lights needed to drop immediately after the last song so she could leave the stage. Fast.

It worked, and although she could hear the crowd calling for more, for the first time in her life Skye didn't care. She collapsed in a chair backstage.

Someone called an ambulance and Skye felt herself being put onto the gurney. She heard a deep voice telling her she'd be okay, but she knew she wouldn't. Something awful was happening. She was afraid she was going to die.

♫ ♫ ♫

A strange assortment of faces swam before Skye's eyes when she opened them the next morning. She remembered getting to the hospital, where they'd poked and prodded and tested her for an eternity. Then, finally, medication. And sleep.

Now she was awake. A man in scrubs stood beside her bed, and behind, her grandmother sat in a chair. Skye smiled. Grandma! Dawdi stood beside her, and next to him, Max and Bo leaned against the wall.

"What's going on?" Skye asked in a small voice.

"You're in kidney failure," the doctor said matter-of-factly.

"Skye my dear," Sue Ann stood up and moved to take her granddaughter's hand. "You'll be all right—just rest for now. Your parents will be here later today, and Angela too. They're on the way."

"Why are they all coming?" Skye's heart flipped. "Am I dying?"

"No, you're not dying," the doctor assured. "But we need to talk about a transplant. You can go for a while on dialysis, but sooner or later you'll need a new kidney."

Skye gulped. This couldn't be happening. One minute she was the focus of thousands of fans' adulation, and less than twelve hours later she was alone, facing a surgeon's knife? No, this couldn't be happening to her.

But, according to the doctor, it was. He explained in very straight-forward terms that her diabetes combined with the abuse she'd put her kidneys through over the years was catching up with her. She'd need to go on dialysis immediately, and it wouldn't hurt to start looking for a donor.

She asked him about her career. He said if she could manage her diet on the road, and arrange for her dialysis, it could work. But she'd have to take good care of herself. Drinking was out. She'd need to maintain her diet, get plenty of rest, and drink lots of fluids. The right kind of fluids, he emphasized again.

Yeah, yeah, yeah, Skye sighed. She could just see herself running to the hospital in every town to drain her kidneys. Please! On the other hand, a transplant? Just when she was at the height of her career! How long would she be down from that? How disgusting. How totally disgusting. Why her? What had she done to deserve this? Why did she have to have diabetes in the first place? Why not Angela too?

Angela. A part of Skye hated her perfect sister and her perfect life. And a part of her—a much larger part—wanted her sister to be there to hold her and tell her everything would be all right.

SKYE

FOUR

ANGELA AND JON walked into Skye's hospital room in Vicksburg at 8:00 that evening. In fact, Skye realized after the initial embraces were over and they were making small talk about their drive from Iowa and her concert the night before, it was exactly 24 hours ago that she'd been singing "You're My Sister." She told Angela, who came over and held her hand.

"I can't believe you're still singing that song," Angela said.

"Hey, it's the one piece of sanity in a crazy concert," Skye said. "And the people expect it."

"We'll have to sing it together again sometime," Angela suggested, and Skye agreed wholeheartedly.

"You look good," Skye noted, admiring her sister's tan face and arms and her wavy, shoulder-length blonde hair. "You look so … healthy."

Angela laughed lightly. "I look like someone who spends a lot of time in the garden," she replied. "You may actually be healthier without the tan, but it just sorta happens on the farm."

No doubt, Skye thought, her eyes skipping to Jon. If Angela looked good, he looked absolutely great. The all-American wholesome farm couple, she smiled.

What Skye really wanted was some time alone with Angela. She knew their parents would be flying in later that evening, and then it would be even harder for the sisters to be alone together. Fortunately, Angela must have felt the same way, because she sent

Jon out to get some supper, and the minute he was gone, she turned to Skye and said, "So, how are you really doing? What's happening, other than this kidney thing?"

Skye's eyes lit up as she told Angela about Bo, going to visit their grandparents and Emma, the Harley ride onto the stage. "It's quite a rush," she said. "Being on a stage with thousands of people screaming your name. Who would have believed it when we were kids?"

"You always dreamed it," Angela said. "And now it's really coming true. And what about this Bo guy?"

"I've known a lot of guys, Angela, but none of them quite like Bo," Skye confided. "He's so at ease with people—everybody from bikers to Dawdi. But hey, I've only known him for two days, and today hardly counts! So don't get any ideas!"

"I'm not the one getting ideas. You are, Skye. I can see it in your eyes and hear it in your voice," Angela teased.

Of course she was right. Skye knew she was attracted to Bo, and she felt the same vibes coming from him too. But he owned a Harley-Davidson store in the middle of Kansas, and she was a traveling rock artist. Not exactly the best dating scenario.

"Well even if I am, there's no way it would work," she said out loud. "As soon as I get on my feet again, I'm hittin' the road. He's stuck here in Kansas."

"You can't be on the road forever," Angela said.

"Well I'm a long way from settling down."

"It's not so bad," Angela smiled.

"Speaking of, where are the boys?"

"At home with Jon's parents. It just made more sense than bringing them along this time. You really should come see us in Iowa."

"I will," Skye promised.

They talked and talked. Skye told Angela about the band, how it felt to do a concert, some of the unusual things that happened to them on the road. Her dream was to have a CD go platinum.

Angela told Skye about her boys, the farm, their church, the children's choir she led and the quartet she sang in. Her dream was to have a multi-ethnic, multi-racial children's choir that could go out on tour.

Jon came back all too soon, but Skye was glad for the time she'd had with Angela. She was watching them eat and talking about how long it takes to get a Harley when she heard familiar voices in the hallway. Seconds later, her parents walked into the room and into her arms.

"Skye, Skye, Skye," Becca repeated, holding her daughter in the hospital bed. Finally she relinquished her place to Ken, who took his turn at greeting Skye. They both hugged Angela and Jon, and then returned to Skye's bedside. "How are you? What's the doctor say?" Ken wanted to know.

"My kidneys bummed out on me and the doctor says I need a transplant," Skye said. "I can be on dialysis for a while, but bottom line is I need to find a kidney. You got any extra?" she tried to joke. "Sure, you can have one of mine, if it's your size," Ken returned.

"Thanks, I'll ask the doc to measure," Skye smiled. "Even if it doesn't fit, I'm glad you're here. Thanks for coming, Mom and Dad."

♫ ♫ ♫

THE NEXT DAY they had the serious donor discussion with the doctor. Angela, Jon, Becca, Ken, Jonas and Sue Ann squeezed into Skye's hospital room, along with the doctor. He didn't waste time in explaining the options. They could put Skye on a waiting list for a donor organ. Or they could look for a relative who might be a match.

Of course they didn't have to look far. Skye felt bad as her eyes automatically met her sister's when the doctor said the words "look for a relative." How could she ask Angela to do that for her?

She didn't have to.

"Jon and I have talked about it already," Angela said quietly. "I'm willing to donate one of mine."

Tears flooded Skye's eyes, and through the mist she could see Angela crying too.

"You don't have to, Angela," Skye said.

"Of course I do. I want to. You're my sister," Angela answered.

The doctor explained they'd have to do some tests to make sure Angela was a match, but the chances were very good. It took only a few minutes to make the arrangements. Angela preferred to have the operation close to home and Skye readily agreed.

"I have six concerts left on this tour," Skye said to the doctor, "Is there any chance I can finish the tour?"

"If you check in for dialysis in every city and take good care of yourself," he answered. "I can help set up those dialysis appointments if you give me your schedule."

And so, with her first dialysis under her belt, Skye left the Vicksburg Hospital the next day. She felt weak but ready to get out of the hospital environment. Her parents, Jon and Angela took her to the motel where the band was staying and said their goodbyes. She thanked them for coming, and said she'd see them all in a month. Then Skye strode out of their world and back into hers.

The band members were watching TV and playing cards in a large suite at the motel. Beer cans and potato chip bags littered the room, and Skye realized it'd been several days since she'd had a drink. She almost reached for a can. No, she told herself, you can't. The thought of having to say no for a month seemed impossible. But she'd try, one "no" at a time.

They needed to hit the road, and Skye made a quick call to Bo at the shop. His deep voice answered the phone, and Skye's heart jumped.

"Bo, it's Skye. I just wanted to thank you for everything, and was wondering if you'd have a minute to drop by and say goodbye. You know, so I can place my order," Skye said.

Bo chuckled deeply. "Skye, I'd love to, but I have a customer in the shop and I really can't leave. I can take your order over the phone though, if you'd like. Which one do you want?"

"Oh, just get me whatever you think I should have," Skye let the disappointment come through her voice. She'd really wanted to see Bo.

"I'll do that—I'll order you the best. And will you be here to pick it up when it gets in?"

"You couldn't keep me away," Skye answered.

"Good. See you then."

"Bye, Bo." Skye hung up and felt a pang in her heart. She'd hoped to see him one more time before they left.

♫ ♫ ♫

THE REST OF THE CONCERT TOUR went well. Skye knew she couldn't drink, and she knew she had to report for her dialysis. She desperately missed the buzz she got from the alcohol, and felt it affected her performance, but the crowds didn't seem to notice.

Her last concert was in Minnesota. And since it was the last concert for a while, the band planned to throw a major party afterwards. Skye had the idea of inviting a dozen fans from the audience, chosen randomly, to party with them. It'd make for great publicity, she figured, and give fans something to look forward to when she went on tour again. It might become a standard part of their road show.

Skye was on that night—she could feel it from the start. Some gigs just felt better than others, and this one worked. When the crowd called for one encore, then a second, she obliged. She wanted to make this one last.

Afterwards they headed for the hotel rooms and pool area they'd reserved for the party. The band members, local radio station DJ's, media, and the twelve lucky winners from the audience gathered around the bar and large buffet of finger foods. Skye got a plateful of veggies and began mingling, telling herself she'd have a blast without drinking.

But she didn't believe it for a minute. And the more she saw others with their drinks, the more she told herself it wouldn't matter this one time. Her surgery was only a week away, so why not? And if something went wrong tonight, the hospital was nearby—she'd just been there in the morning doing the dialysis. She casually sidled up to the bar and asked for a martini. The bartender made one with a flourish, and placed the glass in Skye's trembling hands.

She'd just sip it, she told herself, and her eye caught the gaze of a guy about her age across the room. He was one of the twelve winners, and she felt like he'd been watching her ever since the party started. She was used to being stared at by fans, especially the men. But this guy just wouldn't quit.

Strange, her martini was almost gone already. Might as well get another one before she got too far away from the bar, she reasoned.

An hour, two hours, and the party continued. Sometimes Skye was particularly conscious of the stranger looking at her, and other times he wasn't, or she didn't notice. She was having trouble keeping track of things by now, and she just sort of floated and giggled her way through the room. Suddenly, without meaning to—well she didn't think she meant to—she found herself next to the stranger.

"Hello Skye," he said. "My name's Adrian."

"Hi A-drun," she slurred. "Glad tuh meet yuh."

"Likewise," he said. "You know, something's been driving me crazy all evening. I was at a church convention a few months ago, and there was a lady directing a children's choir that looked just like you. Why, she could have been your twin—you look that much alike. Isn't that wild?"

"Simp-lee wahld," Skye reached out to hold onto Adrian's chair. So, he'd seen Angela. Dear sweet perfect Angela. Her sister who was about to give a kidney to a drunken fool. Shame flooded what little conscience she still had left.

"You don't have a twin sister by chance, do you? I mean, she was the spitting image —"

"No," Skye interrupted. "No, no, no sister. But you know what they say," she paused and gathered her words together, "They say ev'rybody has a twin." She hiccupped loudly and giggled. "Sorry. I gotta go."

Skye made her way into the restroom and slumped onto the toilet. Maybe she'd sit there for awhile. No, she'd go to bed. No, she'd go mingle. She was, after all, the star. She flushed the toilet and leaned against the sink, letting the water run over and over her hands. The face in the mirror was flushed, the eyes bloodshot. She washed her face, and looked again. This time the make-up was streaked. She washed her face again, and yet another time. Finally all of the make-up was gone. If it wasn't for the red puffy eyes, she'd look like Angela—Angela who never wore make-up. Angela!

Oh my God, she cried. How could I tell him I don't have a sister? Skye slid to the floor and sobbed uncontrollably.

SKYE

FIVE

SKYE WOKE UP the morning after the party in the hospital. She wasn't surprised. The drinking binge wasn't exactly good news for her diabetic system and failing kidneys. It took a day to get her stabilized, and then Angela came to pick her up and drive her back to Iowa.

The first thing Skye thought of when she saw Angela was her denial at the party. She felt awful. Absolutely awful. The only way she could think of spending the hours driving with Angela was to stick the party in the back of her mind and bury it there, hoping it would never come out. She had to forget it.

Obviously, Angela knew Skye had messed up by drinking that night, but she didn't talk about it. She filled the driving time with stories of her boys and Jon. She got Skye to start reminiscing about their childhood, and soon they were laughing and giggling together like little girls again. Skye felt so good, so relieved, so positive about life in the presence of Angela. Skye wished they had more time on the road together—just driving and talking.

They pulled into the Swartzendruber yard in central Iowa as the sun was casting a golden glow on the rows and rows of green corn surrounding the farm. The outdoors even smelled like corn, Skye noticed as she stepped out of the car. Her eyes took in the neatly manicured flower beds and garden, the family collie, a mother cat and kittens playing on the sidewalk. What a place to raise a family, she thought. What a life Angela has here.

The happy sounds of young boys could be heard somewhere behind the house, and Angela and Skye followed their ears to see what was going on. There, in the backyard, sat Grandma Swartzendruber in a lawn chair, watching three little half-naked boys running through a water sprinkler. The oldest, bravest one had just managed to squat on top of the sprinkler, much to the amusement of his brothers.

"Well, what have we here?" Angela said, and immediately she was surrounded by three soggy little bodies, holding her from every direction.

"Mommy! Mommy! You're home! Grandma's letting us play in the sprinkler!" the middle one exclaimed.

"I see that," Angela said, laughing. "Maybe we'll have your Aunt Skye help you dry off and put on clean clothes."

Skye smiled at the boys, who seemed a little hesitant to greet her. Well you couldn't blame them—they hardly knew her. Luke was seven—he'd seen her enough to remember her. His grin of recognition said that—plus he was old enough to know that his Aunt Skye made CD's, and that was pretty impressive. Five-year-old Matt was less sure of himself, but he was willing to give anything a try. He studied Skye with his brown eyes, and she wondered what was going on in his young mind.

The youngest one—two-year-old Mark—was definitely shy. In fact, he'd retreated to a safe spot on the side of Angela that wasn't close to Skye, and he wasn't even looking around the corner. He didn't know this stranger, and, Skye realized, it must be really difficult for him to understand why the newcomer looked so much like his mother.

"So, were they good?" Angela asked her mother-in-law Marietta.

"Well, they didn't do anything I haven't seen their father do," Marietta said. Skye guessed her to be in her mid-60's, and doing a good job of keeping up with her grandsons. "Yes, they were fine," she answered. "We had a good time together." She paused and Skye could feel as well as see her head-to-toe gaze. "Hello, Skye, and how are you?"

"I'm okay," Skye said. "Well, as okay as can be expected for someone who's in the market for a new kidney," she tried to joke. She wasn't sure how Marietta felt about her. After all, Skye was taking a kidney from her daughter-in-law and the mother of her grandchildren.

"Yes, I'm sure that isn't any fun. For either of you," Marietta said.

"And speaking of…" Angela jumped in, and Skye was thankful for the rescue. "I guess you're planning on having the boys while I'm in surgery and recovering."

"We sure are. That's Monday morning?"

"Yes, Skye and I need to be there at 7:00."

"We'll be there to see you before the surgery, and we'll take the boys then," Marietta said, standing up from the lawn chair.

"Great. We really appreciate it."

"That's what grandparents are for. I think I'll head home now—see if Joe's dozed off in front of the baseball game on TV."

Angela laughed, thanked her mother-in-law for taking care of the boys, and then ushered them into the house to put on some dry clothes. Skye said she wanted to stay outside and sit by the picnic table and take in the country evening.

♫ ♫ ♫

WHEN ANGELA SUGGESTED they sing together in her church that Sunday, Skye had some misgivings. But there was no way she could say no, so she agreed to sing one of the gospel songs they sang together as teenagers.

"I know it's not very religious, but wouldn't it be fun to sing 'You're My Sister'?" Angela asked.

"Yeah, I'd like that. So what if it's not out of the hymnbook? What are they going to do? Throw you out of the church?"

"Probably not," Angela chuckled. "Let's do it."

Ken and Becca arrived late Saturday night to be with their daughters. They planned to stay through the surgery and until both women were well on the way to recovery. It was good to see them again so soon, Skye realized, but it reminded her of how far apart they'd grown. And it made her sad.

The twins walked into First Mennonite Church that Sunday morning, along with Jon, the boys, Ken and Becca; and in true small-town fashion, the heads turned. Many of the church members had heard about Skye, but most of them hadn't seen her. Having a celebrity in their midst who happened to be the twin sister of one of their most loved members, plus the reason for them all being together—well, it would be something to talk about for awhile at the local hair salons and coffee shop.

Skye felt conspicuous. She'd rather be walking into a coliseum full of thousands of people waiting to see and hear her than into this church. She knew it was strange for her to feel that way. After all, she'd grown up in a church. But the last fifteen years had led her in a very different direction. Now she felt ashamed and guilty walking into the church, knowing people were looking at her and talking about her. She sure was glad she'd worn one of Angela's long denim skirts and blouses. At least the way she was dressed wasn't adding fuel to the fire.

The service reminded her a lot of the church she and Angela grew up in, and Skye began to relax. When it came time for their songs, Angela led the way to the stage. They picked up their guitars and stood together behind the podium. Feels like old times, Skye thought, smiling. It would be fun to perform with her sister again.

And the first verse was fun. Their voices blended perfectly, like they always had, with Angela taking the soprano line and Skye harmonizing on alto. But when it came time for the chorus, the words began to hit Skye hard.

With God on our side, we made it you and I,
And we wouldn't change a single thing
for all the stars in the sky.
And if tomorrow comes too fast
Make each moment last today
And the good Lord will remain to lead the way.

Skye's heart began to pound. She was scared. Scared to go

into surgery the next day. For the first time, the seriousness of the transplant operations sank into her soul. *If tomorrow comes too fast.* What if she died tomorrow? Or the next day? Oh God no! She wasn't ready to die!

The performer in Skye didn't let her turmoil show, and she sang automatically—but with the same intensity she put into the song at every concert. She could be automatically intense with this song, and she could see the effect she and Angela were leaving on the listeners. The people of First Mennonite were eating it up, religious or not. Any other time, she would have gotten a kick out of seeing their faces absorbing the music. But this morning her nerves were suddenly strung tight—tighter than the strings on her guitar. And it had nothing to do with singing.

The time for sharing in the service came, and Skye shifted uncomfortably in the pew. Angela had told her the deacons and pastor wanted to have an anointing service for them before the surgery. Skye wasn't at all sure about that, but how could she say no? If it was important to Angela, she'd do it for her. And she supposed it couldn't do any harm, other than the embarrassment of being in front of the church, being watched.

The pastor asked Angela and Skye to come to the front, and to kneel. Skye's legs shook all the way. For heaven's sake, get a hold of yourself, she thought.

They knelt together on the stage. The pastor explained that anointing was a way of calling on God to be with someone for a specific purpose or mission, and this would be a time to invite God's healing presence for Angela and Skye during and after the transplant. He invited anyone from the congregation to come stand with Angela and Skye, and within minutes the twins were surrounded. Young and old, children who ran up and seniors who walked very slowly—Skye was amazed at how many people came forward. She began to wonder if there weren't more people on the stage than in the pews.

Ken and Becca, Jon and the boys, Marietta and Joe were there of course, along with many people Skye didn't know. The pastor stood in front of Angela—he was holding a small bottle of oil. He tipped the bottle onto his fingertip, and then touched Angela's forehead lightly with the oil.

"Angela, I anoint you in the name of our Lord Jesus Christ. May the Holy Spirit anoint your body and soul with power from above."

Angela bowed her head, and Skye knew it was her turn. She lifted her face and closed her eyes. She could feel people's hands touching her shoulders, her back, and then she felt the touch of a fingertip on her forehead, and the warm oil. "Skye, I anoint you in the name of our Lord Jesus Christ. May the Holy Spirit anoint your body and soul with power from above."

Skye didn't know what to expect. Maybe she'd hoped for the fear to be gone. It wasn't. What she did feel was … loved. As she and Angela stood up, those around them hugged them, then silently filed back to their seats. Skye followed Angela back to their row and sat down. She realized she could cry, but she wouldn't. She looked at Angela. She was.

♫ ♫ ♫

THAT EVENING, while Jon played with the boys in the yard, Skye and Angela went for a walk. Skye needed to talk. Her apprehension had grown ever since the song that morning. The anointing made her feel loved and supported, but it didn't take away the fear. She wondered how Angela was feeling. Was she scared too?

The July evening air hung heavy over the twins as they walked along the paved country road. It didn't take long until Skye was wiping the sweat from her forehead, and she could feel it dripping down her back.

"It's getting close," she said to Angela. "I didn't really think about it until we sang this morning. The part about 'if tomorrow comes too fast' really hit me. Now I'm scared. Aren't you?"

Angela turned toward Skye, and the look on her face was different than anything Skye could remember seeing from her sister. "I'm terrified, Skye," Angela said, and suddenly there were tears rimming her eyes. "It seemed easy to say yes at the time, but not right now. I'm sorry. I know I shouldn't even be thinking like this."

Skye felt as if her heart was being ripped in two. Her life depended on her sister, but what right did she have to ask Angela to go through with this? None. None at all.

"You don't have to do it," Skye stopped, her eyes filling. She reached for Angela and they clung to each other. "We can call it off," Skye sobbed. "We really can."

"No," Angela sniffled. "No, we're going through with it. We're going to be okay. It's just nerves, that's all."

They separated and slowly continued walking, each lost in their own thoughts.

♫ ♫ ♫

THE DRIVE TO THE HOSPITAL the next morning was unusually quiet. The boys were still groggy with sleep, Jon never was a big talker, and even Angela wasn't making attempts at conversation. Skye knew she personally hadn't slept much, and Angela looked tired and strung-out too. Oh well, Skye thought, they'd get to catch up on their sleep after the surgery.

Ken and Becca had spent the night at Joe and Marietta's house, and they were at the hospital already when the Swartzendrubers and Skye arrived. They all stood together in the lobby, making small talk, waiting for instructions on what to do next. Finally a nurse in scrubs arrived.

"Okay, I guess this is where I take Skye and Angela with me," she said. "You can say your goodbyes now, and you'll be able to see them in ICU within 24 hours."

Skye held onto Ken, then Becca, for a long time. When she finally let go, she saw that Angela was still in the arms of her husband and sons. Oh God, Skye prayed, please please please let everything go all right. If not for my sake, for hers. Please God!

♫ ♫ ♫

IT WAS TIME. The nurses and doctors had done all the final health checks, and everything looked good for the transplant. Skye and Angela lay on movable hospital beds, ready to be wheeled into surgery. Skye's heart pounded. She looked over at Angela and their eyes met.

"Hey Skye," Angela's hand patted her lower back. "This one's for you."

SKYE

SIX

SOMETHING WAS WRONG. Horribly awfully terribly wrong. Skye opened her eyes, and tried to focus her mind on her surroundings. Yes, the hospital. A kidney transplant. Pain. People around her. Her family.

Her mother and father were standing beside her bed. That's what was wrong. Their faces. She'd never seen their faces look like that before.

"Skye," Becca said. "How're you feeling?"

Skye heard the words, but the only thing that registered was her mother's red swollen eyes. She felt like she'd been punched in the stomach, and her wind knocked out. She felt her heart drop.

"Mom? Dad?"

Her parents both reached for her hands, and Skye knew. She knew without hearing, and she didn't want to hear. No, don't say it. Don't tell me. Oh please say it isn't true!

"Skye," it was her father's broken voice this time. "Angela … she … she had a reaction to the anesthetic. We … we lost her." Ken's face crumpled, and Skye closed her eyes.

No. NO, NO, NO!! Skye sreamed inside of her self, and her heart tore from top to bottom. It could not have happened! Not Angela! Angela couldn't have died! NO!

Anger surged through her. She opened her eyes again and stared at her parents. "What happened?"

"We don't really know. They're just saying it was one of those one in a million cases. Anesthetic is always a risk," Becca said, reaching into her purse for a tissue. The action brought something to Skye's mind.

"Mom, please, bring me my bandanna," Skye's voice cracked. Then the sobs took over, and while her parents held her in the hospital bed, Skye cried.

She cried for herself, and the sudden incredible emptiness in her heart. She cried for Jon and the little boys who'd waved goodbye to their mother—forever. She cried for her parents. She cried for the total unfairness of it all. She cried because, if anyone should die, it should have been her. Angela didn't deserve to die. Now she was gone, and Skye was left alone. Alone and broken. She cried because she didn't know if she wanted to live.

Finally the sobs subsided. Skye knew they would be back. Many times. For now, a dull aching pain settled into her soul.

♫ ♫ ♫

THE TRANSPLANT ITSELF had gone well. Angela's healthy kidney was functioning well inside Skye, and there were no signs of rejection. The doctors didn't anticipate any problems, but Skye could hardly think about her own health. The physical pain she felt from the surgery was something they could prescribe medication for—and they had. The meds helped shroud her emotional hurt as well, but nothing covered the stark shocking reality. Angela was gone. Just like that. Gone.

When Becca brought Skye her red bandanna, it triggered a new round of grief. She simply couldn't understand. Nothing made sense. Why? Why did it happen? Why to Angela? Why to the mother of three little boys who needed her desperately? Why to someone with her gifts with music and people? She had so much to offer the world!

Angela had so totally and unselfishly offered her kidney to Skye, and in doing so, she'd given up her life! All for Skye! The enormity of the sacrifice swamped Skye's mind, and her body shook as the realization washed over her again and again. It just didn't make any sense!

Later that day, her room began to fill with people. Her parents, grandparents, Jon and his parents, and the pastor at First Mennonite Church—they were all there, along with a couple she didn't know. Funeral home directors. They had a funeral to plan.

"Skye, this is Mike and Nancy Miller," Ken said quietly. "From the funeral home back in Elm City."

"Yeah," Skye said.

"First, let me say that this is extremely hard for us, even though it's what we do for a living," Mike Miller said. "We knew Angela. She was one of the most wonderful women in our community. I don't know what to say except that we grieve with you, and we'll do everything we can to help you through this time," he paused and swallowed hard. Reaching into a small briefcase, he brought out a stack of sheets and handed them out. "This is a list of things that we need to be thinking about."

Skye scanned the piece of paper. Date. Time. Place. Order of service. Casket. Pallbearers. The words on the list began to swim.

"Thursday morning would be a possible time," the pastor suggested, and silent nods in the room gave assent. "Like at 10:00?" More nods.

"I'll never forget Ken's father's funeral," Becca spoke up. "It was so uplifting. I'd never been to a funeral that celebrated a person's life. Angela's should be that way too."

"I agree," Jon said. "It will be very hard, but I agree."

Skye listened as they planned. They asked her for ideas, but she had none. She couldn't even be there. And she couldn't make herself think about the elements of her sister's funeral. Not without crying again. And she refused to cry again. Not with everyone else there.

They were going on with the list of things to do. Mike had just read the words "Notification of friends and relatives."

"Most of them are in Iowa, Kansas and Pennsylvania," Ken said, and then a shadow crossed his weary face. "Except ..." he looked at Becca, then Skye. "Except for Andrea. We don't know where she is."

The room grew quiet, except for the hum of the machines

hooked up to Skye. Skye felt anger and sorrow cresting in her again. Their biological mother. Andrea—who showed up at their graduation years ago and then disappeared from sight. Andrea—who dumped twin daughters in the laps of strangers. Andrea—their birth mother who didn't know about the death of her daughter. Skye hated her. For the moment, she hated her.

"Well it's not like she's been banging down the door to see us," Skye broke the silence in the room. She could see surprise on some of the faces at her bitter words, and she didn't really care. It was true.

"No, but don't we owe it to her to try to find her and let her know?" Ken said.

"And how are you going to do that in two days?" Skye shot back.

"I don't know," Ken shrugged his shoulders. "Last we knew, she was in Florida."

"Fifteen years ago!" Skye exploded. The force of her words hurt all the way down to her incision, and she winced.

"There are ways," Mike said.

"No," Skye said. "I don't want you to look for her."

She meant it. Totally. What right did her biological mother have to invade her life now, of all times? She didn't need her. She didn't want her. She'd just lost the closest person to her on earth, and she didn't need the added pain of meeting a mother who'd abandoned her. No way.

"Okay Skye, we won't. It's all right," Becca said. "We all have enough to deal with right now." She looked at Ken, and Skye knew the message that passed between them. Just let it go.

Skye was tired by the time the planning was finally completed. Her medication had her drifting in and out, and she wasn't even sure when the last person left. She fell into an exhausted sleep.

♫ ♫ ♫

THE FLOWERS STARTED ARRIVING soon after the surgery. The media had picked up the story and plastered it across the nation. The tragic death of one twin in the process of donating a kidney to the other was news in and of itself. To have the donor be a Christian children's choir director and the recipient a rock star—well it didn't get much better than that, as far as the media was concerned. The family tried to reach all close friends and relatives before the story got out, but there was still the fear of someone close to Angela reading it when they picked up the morning paper. At any rate, Skye's fans were finding out, and flowers began to flood her room with fragrance. She noticed, but she didn't care.

Cards came too. Someone read them all to her—either a family member or a nurse. Many were from people she didn't know. It was nice to know they were thinking about her. It felt awful to be in a position of needing comfort.

Wednesday morning, the florist delivered another load. There wasn't any more space available in her room.

"Put them in the waiting room. Take them to other patients—anything," Skye said flatly. "Just leave the cards."

She flipped through the cards half-heartedly. She stopped short at the last one.

> *Skye, I am so sorry to hear about your sister. My thoughts are with you. Bo*

Skye read the card over and over again. She wondered which flowers he'd sent. There wasn't any way to find out now—the cards were all separated from the bouquets. That was a stupid thing to do, she thought, and the tears that had been so near the surface for two days came again.

♫ ♫ ♫

THEY SAID THEY HATED TO LEAVE HER ALONE, and Skye knew it was true. The family members had all gone to Elm City for the evening to be in the funeral home as friends and neighbors came to pay their respects. She was alone in her room with the machines, the pain, and the flowers. She was on an IV that allowed her to dispense her pain meds when she needed them. Within certain limits, of course. What she needed was a good drink, Skye thought. She flipped on the televison and cruised through the channels. Nothing worth watching. She checked the time to see when she could give herself another dose. Yeah, she could do it now. Maybe she'd go to sleep. Anything to pass the hours until....

Until what? Until the funeral was over? Until she could leave the hospital? Until she could hit the road again? Until she could face the rest of her life without Angela?

Skye slept restlessly, and dreamed. She dreamed of their high school graduation. Singing together with Angela. How eager she was to leave it all behind—the small town, Pennsylvania, her family, even her sister. As long as they were in the background, that was great. But she had bigger and better places to go. She dreamed of sitting behind Bo on his Harley, riding into an arena of screaming fans. Only they weren't calling her name. They were calling Angela! Angela! Angela!

"Andrea. Tell her my name's Andrea!" Skye woke with a start. A woman was arguing with the security guard outside her door. They'd had to put one there to allow only family members inside the room.

"Tell her it's Andrea—her mother!" the woman's voice said forcefully.

"I'm sorry, ma'am, but we know her mother and it isn't you," the guard was saying.

Skye went cold. Her mother. Her mother Andrea was standing outside her door.

SKYE

SEVEN

"LET HER IN," Skye told the security guard outside her hospital room. She turned her head and watched as Andrea entered. A woman about her size with short red hair flecked with gray. The same green eyes that Skye saw in her mirror. So. This was her mother.

"Hello, Skye," Andrea said. "I … I read about Angela in the paper. I … I'm so sorry."

Andrea was leaning against the wall, as if afraid to come close to Skye. She hung her head as she said, "I'm sorry it's taken me so long to come. I'm sorry for everything. You've got to believe me. I am!" She looked up at Skye, her eyes pleading.

Skye wanted to hold her mother and kick her out of the room all at the same time.

"Why didn't you come to our graduation party after you talked to Dad?" Skye wanted to know.

"I was afraid. I was afraid of all those people, and making a scene. I didn't want to ruin your party."

Skye grinned bitterly. "Well, it was ruined all right, 'cause we kept waiting for you."

"I'm sorry. What else can I say?"

"Why haven't you looked us up since then? Why did it take Angela's death to get you here?"

Andrea walked closer to the bed, her face begging Skye to understand her heart. "Because I always felt so guilty about leaving you. Because I didn't want to upset the lives you made for yourselves. Because I was afraid it would be like this—that you would hate me. It was easier not to see you."

Skye was quiet. She hated to admit it, but Andrea had a point.

The phone rang, and Skye reached over to pick it up.

"Hello."

"Hi Skye, how're you doing?" Becca's voice asked.

"I'm okay," Skye said automatically. What could she say? That her biological mother had just walked into the room?

"What are you doing?" Becca wanted to know.

"Not much, Mom."

"We'll be there as soon as we can tomorrow afternoon," Becca said. "We'll bring a tape of the funeral."

"Thanks. Fine. I'll see you then."

"You get some rest and keep healing," Becca was trying to sound cheerful, Skye thought.

"I will. See you then. Goodbye."

Skye looked at Andrea, who had backed up to the wall again, and then she looked at the phone. "That was my mom," she said simply, and Andrea nodded.

An uncomfortable silence hung between them as the monitors and machines beeped and purred, and finally Skye couldn't take it any longer.

"Look Andrea … Mother. I need some time, and I'm tired. Could you come back tomorrow evening? When Mom and Dad are here? Could we just all talk together?"

Andrea nodded again. "Could I … could I just give you a hug?" she said softly.

Skye agreed. Her mother walked the few steps to the bed and wrapped her arms around Skye. Dry-eyed, Skye thanked her for coming and said she'd see her tomorrow. Andrea said she'd be back, and as she walked to the door, she turned back and added, "I promise." Then she was gone.

♫ ♫ ♫

TOO MUCH. Too much to handle for one mind and one body

in three days. Skye desperately wanted to escape the hurt from the surgery, Angela's death, and now the appearance of Andrea. In the past, alcohol had helped her make escapes. Now she didn't have that, and the lack of a crutch seemed unbearable. If it wasn't for the meds soothing the edges of her pain, she wouldn't know what she would do.

She watched a movie on televison, drifting in and out of a medication-induced drowsiness. She woke when the evening news was on and flipped the switch. A nurse came in to check her vitals and IV, and then left again. Skye fell back asleep.

She woke up early in the morning. It had to be early, because the sun was just starting to shine on her window blinds. She stared at it awhile, still half-asleep. Interesting, she mused. Somehow the light seemed to be coming from the inside of the blinds rather than the window behind it. She closed her eyes again, and then she heard her name.

"Skye."

Her eyes flew open. It was Angela's voice! Her heart pounding, she looked toward the window—where the voice came from. A hazy, shimmering white form stood there and Skye gasped out loud. "Angela?"

Angela seemed to float-walk toward the bed, and Skye sat upright, then froze in place.

"Skye, it's okay," Angela said. "I just had to come say goodbye, and tell you that it's going to be okay."

"But … You …" Skye stuttered.

"I know. I'm gone. From earth anyway. But Skye!" Angela's face shone. "Heaven is so awesome! You can't imagine how beautiful it is!"

Skye finally found her voice. "Angela, I don't know what to do. I feel so lost without you."

Angela moved closer. Skye was sure Angela wasn't close enough to touch her, but a warmth began in her chest and spread slowly throughout her being. "You still have me inside of you," Angela said. "And God too, if you ask. If you give God a place in your heart. And you have people who love you."

People who love her.

"She came today—our mother," Skye said.

"I know. Skye, you have to forgive her. You have to give yourself and our mother the gift of love without conditions. It's the only way, Skye, believe me."

As Skye watched, Angela seemed to fade back toward the wall and the window. No, she couldn't leave. Not yet!

"Angela! Please!" Skye cried.

"I love you, Skye, and I'll always be inside of you." Skye heard the words but the image was gone. The light on the window blinds grew, and suddenly the morning sun shone through.

♫ ♫ ♫

SKYE STARED AT THE WORDS on the tablet in front of her. She had no idea how long she'd been writing. It could have been minutes, or hours. She only knew that the song in front of her was an ending, and a beginning.

"SISTERS"
(Angela's Song)

VERSE ONE
Even though we were twins and very small,
we were never like each other at all.
You wanted to stay close to home,
and I had a passion to roam and roam.
Somehow your world was tidy and safe,
but my path took me to another kind of place.
You were a caterpillar crawling on the ground,
the blue Skye of my name my butterfly wings found.

CHORUS
Sisters, our paths have parted now,
sisters, how can I go on—I'll have to find out how
to keep travelin' this road,

when you have left me and taken a part of my soul,
oh Angela, Angela…

VERSE TWO
Older, you had babies and were a farmer's wife,
I became a rock star and traveled the skies.
You never left the boundaries of our childhood,
living a secure life, I never could…
But even though you've left the earth, you're still not too far
to know my music is longing to reach you heart.
It's never too late to share our lives,
don't leave me now to fly alone in the sky…

CHORUS
Sisters, our paths have parted now,
sisters, how can I go on—I don't know how…
I can't keep travelin' this road,
when you have left and taken a part of my soul,
oh Angela, Angela…

BRIDGE
Angela, when you were on earth with me,
you finally made me see,
it was okay to let down and trust,
you gave me so much that you died from your love.

VERSE THREE
I never was as sure about God as you,
no matter how far I searched I never quite knew,
if God was listening to all my songs of life,
or if they touched his heart and if he cried?
But this one's for you, Angela, I know you're up above,
tell heaven I'm singing you a song of my love,
And until I get there to share that home,
always know you have a part of my soul.

CHORUS
Sisters, our paths have parted now,
sisters, I will go on—I do know how ...
I can keep travelin' this road,
even though you've left and taken a part of my soul,
oh Angela, Angela.

"Sisters" (Angela's Song) © 1997 Laurie L. Oswald. For information on ordering a tape of the song, *see page 186.*

EPILOGUE

JONAS

IT'S BEEN A MONTH, and many times I still can't believe Angela's gone. Of course it's hit Skye the hardest. They were twins. The bond that tied them together from the womb will never break.

Maybe that's what's going on inside of Skye. I got a letter from her the other day—she's at home with Ken and Becca, recovering, getting her strength back. In her letter, she said she'd been thinking a lot about her life, and what to do next.

> *Dawdi, I'm beginning to realize there's more to life than fame and money. Angela knew that. She gave her life to her family, her church, her children's choir. Then she gave her life for me.*

It still hurts. It hurts bad. I remember giving my bandanna to Skye when she was a little girl, so she could use it when she needed to cry. Well, I've used my worn bandannas more in the last month than I care to count. I know it's normal, but I'm ready for the grieving to pass. Skye thinks Angela knew. She wrote about it in her letter.

> *Angela told me the night before she died that she was scared. I wonder if she had a feeling she might not*

make it through the surgery. Whether or not Angela knew she was going to die, I'm beginning to know a few things about life. I can't go back on the road. Something has to change. I don't know how, or what I'll do. I'm giving up one dream, but I'm not sure what to replace it with.

I do know I can't forget the afternoon when Bo and I rode his Harley to visit you and Emma. Maybe, when I'm up to it, I'll come to Kansas and do that again. If I learn to drive the cycle, would you go for a ride with me?

Wouldn't that be a sight—me, an old Amish minister, riding behind Skye on a motorcycle. That would turn some heads in Wellsford!

One more thing, Dawdi. I want to thank you for the bandanna you gave me so long ago. It's been with me through a lot, and soaked up many tears since Angela died. But it also reminds me of you, and those are good feelings. I love you,

Skye

I wish she were here. I wish I could give Skye a Dawdi-hug and tell her it'll be okay. God is faithful—I know. I have a long life full of proof. And of memories. Memories of two little girls catching lightning bugs, playing in the mud, and one blonde green-eyed angel learning to play the harmonica.

The End

AFTERWORD

FROM THE AUTHORS

THE BOOK YOU HAVE JUST READ IS FICTION, but it is based on some things that have really happened to us—things we don't understand to this day. Here's the story:

For a number of years following our marriage, Maynard had a recurring dream. He was driving along the road, came to a curve, and a pregnant girl was standing there, waiting for a ride. He picked her up, she gave birth to twin daughters, and she left. We raised the girls.

Maynard didn't tell Carol about the dream for a long time, and when he did, it was one of those "Isn't that strange" things we shared with a few close friends and family members.

One day Maynard and a hired hand were driving their small pickup on one of their business trips. They saw a girl along the side of the road, waiting for a ride. They didn't stop for her, but went on into town and did some business there. They left town, going a different direction. They came upon a curve in the road—and the girl was there again. Apparently she'd caught a ride that far. Maynard was starting to feel just a little bit weird at that point, and decided to pick her up. They did, and although it wasn't obvious, she said she was pregnant. She also mentioned that she herself was a twin, and she was running away from an abusive boyfriend.

Maynard gave her a ride as far as he could, and gave her our phone number. She called the next day, wondering if we had a job for her. We didn't, and we haven't heard from her since.

But to this day, we tell ourselves that if the doorbell rings and twin girls are standing there asking to come live with us, we'd have to say, "We've been expecting you."

Several years after the incident with the hitchhiker, we decided to write a fictional book about a teenager growing up Amish. All of Carol's writing up until that point had been non-fiction. She didn't know if she could just "make things up." We were talking about that one day, and Maynard said the never-to-be-forgotten words, "You mean when you're driving down the road you don't have stories in your head? You don't have pictures playing in your mind?"

"Of course not," Carol said. "What in the world are you talking about?"

What Maynard revealed that day was that he often has stories flying through his mind, and that they just "happen." One of the continuing stories involves the twins from the dream. They grow up. They are wonderful musicians as children and as adults, but very different. One settles in Iowa as a farm wife and one is a rock star who drives a Harley-Davidson on stage.

Sound familiar? Obviously. Because we decided to incorporate that story into the first book of the Skye series. But there's more.

Maynard kept saying that "This book is going to be heavy." And Carol believed him, but she wasn't exactly sure what part was heavy. Of course the circumstances of the twins' arrival was unusual and powerful. But she didn't know where the book was going. What was the plot? How did it end?

Several weeks before Christmas 1996, Carol was out jogging when the meaning of *Twins* hit her. She knows exactly where she was on the road when it seems the Holy Spirit said "Hello! Carol! About *Twins*..."

That was only one of the many times when we were amazed at how the pieces of *Twins* came together. Here's another example. We needed twin girls to pose for the cover. We talked to people about it, and references from two different communities told us about the same set of twins. We went to see them—they live just a few miles from us but we didn't know them. Perfect. They looked like what Maynard had imagined. And then, in passing, we heard their birth date. It's December 25.

Sometimes we just walk around shaking our heads. But mostly, we thank a God who chooses to be involved in people's lives in powerful, subtle, exciting, wonderful ways.

— *Carol Duerksen and Maynard Knepp*

Coming Next:

HEARTBEAT

Book 2—Skye Series

(CASSETTE TAPE)

"YOU'RE MY SISTER" and "Sisters" are performed on this cassette by a young up-and-coming artist from rural Haven, Kansas named Shannon Smith. At the age of 13, Shannon heard country singer Martina McBride in concert, and decided then and there she wanted to get into performing. Less than a year later, singing McBride's song "Independence Day," Shannon claimed first place in Hutchinson's talent contest held in conjunction with its HutchFest Extravaganza.

In a story about Shannon, the Hutchinson News stated "She could be the next LeAnn Rimes." Find out for yourself as you hear her sing the stirring songs from *TWINS.*

ALSO INCLUDED ON THE CASSETTE:

- Sing-a-long trax version of the *Twins* music, as co-written by Jake Schmidt and Matthew Jordan ("You're My Sister") and Laurie Oswald ("Sisters").

- Maynard Knepp, co-author of *Twins,* tells "The Story Behind the Story"—an inside peek at how he and his wife Carol Duerksen created the Jonas Series and now the Skye Series.

- A story from another newly released book from Willow-Spring Downs—*Slickfester Dude Tells Bedtime Stories.* This book of true animal stories is told by Slickfester Dude, a very observant black cat on Maynard and Carol's farm. Each story ends with a poignant lesson on life, and will be heart-warming for adults as well as children.

For information on how to order the *Twins* cassette or any of the books from WillowSpring Downs, see order forms on the next pages.

Twins Cassette Tape
Order Form

Please rush _____ copy/copies of the *Twins* cassette to the following address:

Name ____

Address ____

City ______________________ State ______________

Zip ____________ Phone # __________________________

____ Cassette(s) at $9.95 = Total $ ______

Add 6.9% KS Sales Tax ______

Add $3 Shipping/Handling for 1st copy ______

Add $.50 Shipping/Handling each add'l copy ______

TOTAL ENCLOSED $ ______

Sorry, we can't accept C.O.D. orders

Make check or money order payable to: J & M Artist Management and mail, along with this order form to:

J & M Artist Management
PO Box 355
Hutchinson, KS 67505-0355
Fax: (316) 665-6141

Any questions or requests for more information can be sent to the above address.

Please allow 4-6 weeks for delivery.

OTHER BOOKS FROM
WILLOWSPRING DOWNS

JONAS SERIES

The Jonas Series was the brainchild of Maynard Knepp, a popular speaker on the Amish culture who grew up in an Amish family in central Kansas. Knepp and his wife Carol Duerksen, a freelance writer, collaborated to produce their first book, *Runaway Buggy*, released in October, 1995. The resounding success of that book encouraged them to continue, and the series grew to four books within 18 months. The books portray the Amish as real people who face many of the same decisions, joys and sorrows as everyone else, as well as those that are unique to their culture and tradition. Written in an easy-to-read style that appeals to a wide range of ages and diverse reader base — from elementary age children to folks in their 90s, from dairy farmers to PhDs — fans of the Jonas Series are calling it captivating, intriguing, can't-put-it-down reading.

RUNAWAY BUGGY

This book sweeps the reader into the world of an Amish youth trying to find his way "home." Not only does *Runaway Buggy* pull back a curtain to more clearly see a group of people, but it intimately reveals the heart of one of their sons struggling to become a young man all his own.

HITCHED

With *Hitched*, the second installment in the Jonas Series, the reader struggles with Jonas as he searches for the meaning of Christianity and tradition, and feels his bewilderment as he recognizes that just as there are Christians who are not Amish, there are Amish who are not Christians.

PREACHER

Book Three in the Jonas Series finds Jonas Bontrager the owner of a racehorse named Preacher, and facing dilemmas that only his faith can explain, and only his faith can help him endure.

BECCA

The fourth book in the Jonas Series invites readers to see the world through the eyes of Jonas Bontrager's 16-year-old daughter Becca, as she asks the same questions her father did, but in her own fresh and surprising ways.

Slickfester Dude Tells Bedtime Stories

Life Lessons from our Animal Friends

by Carol Duerksen *(& Slickfester Dude)*

WillowSpring Downs is not only a publishing company — it's also a 120-acre piece of paradise in central Kansas that's home to a wide assortment of animals. Slickfester Dude, a black cat with three legs that work and one that doesn't, is one of those special animals. In a unique book that only a very observant cat could write, Slickfester Dude tells Carol a bedtime story every night — a story of life among the animals and what it can mean for everyone's daily life. This book will delight people from elementary age and up because the short stories are told in words that both children and adults can understand and take to heart. Along with strong, sensitive black and white story illustrations, the book includes Slickfester Dude's Photo Album of his people and animal friends at WillowSpring Downs.

ORDER FORM

Jonas Series: *($9.95 each* **OR** *2 or more, any title mix, $10 each, we pay shipping.)*

______ copy/copies of *Runaway Buggy*

______ copy/copies of *Hitched*

______ copy/copies of *Preacher*

______ copy/copies of *Becca*

______ Jonas Series—all 4 books, $36.50

For more information or to be added to our mailing list, call or fax us on our toll-free number
1-888-551-0973

Skye Series:

______ copy/copies of *Twins* @ $9.95 each

Other:

______ copy/copies of *Slickfester Dude Tells Bedtime Stories* @ $9.95 each

Name ______________________________

Address ______________________________

City ____________________ State ______________

Zip ______________ Phone # ____________________

____ Book(s) at $9.95 = Total $ ______

Add $3 postage/handling if only one copy ______

SPECIAL PRICE = Buy 2 or more, pay $10 each and we'll pay the shipping.

Total enclosed $ ______

Make checks payable to WillowSpring Downs and mail, along with this order form, to the following address:

WillowSpring Downs
Route 2, Box 31
Hillsboro, KS 67063-9600